MURDER, SHE WROTE

THE MURDER OF SHERLOCK HOLMES
A NOVEL BY JAMES ANDERSON

Based on the Universal television series "Murder She Wrote"
Created by Peter S. Fischer and Richard Levinson & William Link
Adapted from the episode "The Murder of Sherlock Holmes"
Teleplay by Peter S. Fischer
Story by Richard Levinson & William Link and Peter S. Fischer

AVON
PUBLISHERS OF BARD, CAMELOT, DISCUS AND FLARE BOOKS

AVON BOOKS
A division of
The Hearst Corporation
1790 Broadway
New York, New York 10019

Chapter One

"OF course, her uncle killed her," said Mrs. Fletcher.

Mrs. Thompson stared. "Oh, surely not!"

"Whatever makes you say that?" asked Mrs. Hoey.

"It just seems obvious. I mean, when the uncle showed up after the party wearing a different tie, he'd obviously changed it for a reason. And there was the phone call from the coroner—he couldn't have known about that unless he'd overheard the doctor talking to the priest."

Mrs. Thompson and Mrs. Hoey looked bemused. "Say that again," demanded Mrs. Hoey.

"Slowly," pleaded Mrs. Thompson.

"It's really quite simple." Mrs. Fletcher took a deep breath. Then she paused and frowned. "Or have I been completely bamboozled? Surely not . . ."

She stood up suddenly. "Well, there's one way to find out."

"Jessica, what are you going to do?"

"Ask the director."

Jessica Fletcher started to make her way down the aisle of the small theatre. Her friends followed her hastily.

"He'll never tell you," said Mrs. Thompson.

"Not perhaps in so many words," said Jessica placidly.

The director had risen from his seat in the first row of the otherwise empty auditorium. He was now haranguing some unhappy-looking actors who had formed a small group at the front of the stage. He made a gesture of dismissal and they shuffled off into the wings. The director turned and saw Jessica and her friends approaching. He scowled.

"Ladies, this is a private rehearsal. No outsiders."

Jessica raised her eyebrows. "Excuse me, Mr. Cellini, but you did ask us to meet you here."

He looked disbelieving. "Now, why would I do a thing like that? I don't even know you!"

"We're the refreshment committee," Mrs. Thompson explained.

"From the PTA," added Mrs. Hoey.

"Oh." This information did not seem to fill Mr. Cellini with intense delight. "The cookie ladies," he said wearily. "Look, see me after the rehearsal, will you? We've still got two acts to get through—and we open tomorrow night."

"Mr. Cellini, I just love the show," said Mrs. Thompson. "It's so . . . so mystifying."

"Yeah, well, that's the idea." Mr. Cellini looked at his watch.

"And so exciting to have a pre-Broadway premiere right here in a little place like Cabot Cove," added Mrs. Hoey.

"Well, there won't be any premiere, let alone a Broadway run, if I don't get the thing right. So if you'll excuse me . . ."

He moved away and started to climb the short flight of steps to the stage.

"And I'm sure no one will guess that the uncle is the killer," Jessica called after him.

Halfway up the steps Mr. Cellini froze. For a full five

seconds he stood quite still. Jessica and her friends surveyed his back with interest. Then he turned slowly.

"*What* did you say?" exclaimed Mr. Cellini.

Lois Thompson gave a giggle. "Poor Mr. Cellini. I thought he was going to have a fit—once you'd convinced him you hadn't read the script, Jess."

"He can see his dreams of a Broadway run fading fast, I guess," said Eleanor Hoey.

Jessica gave a sigh. "Yes, I'm afraid that play's got about as much chance of a successful Broadway run as I have of swimming the English Channel. I felt a bit mean—but on the other hand, it's surely better that flaws be pointed out now, rather than have professional critics tear the play apart publicly."

"Well, I don't know," said Lois thoughtfully. "I enjoyed it. I think it might do quite well."

"And after all," said Eleanor, "neither Lois nor I guessed the end. It's just that you're so good at mysteries, Jessica. Even Agatha Christie and Ellery Queen didn't always fool you."

"A natural flair," said Lois. "Just like Miss Marple."

Jessica Fletcher was a widow in her mid-fifties. She was energetic, intelligent, intensely interested in people—and had the happy knack of being able to get on easily with folk of every age and social background. She had a strong sense of justice, a deep dislike of sham in any form, an ever-present urge to help those who needed it, and a belief in speaking her mind. Any tendency these characteristics might have had to give her the reputation of a do-gooding busybody was, however, offset by a wicked sense of fun and humor—which had once or twice come close to getting her into hot water. She was attractive, dressed smartly in a conservative manner—being much given to tweed suits and sweaters—and, when her services were required, worked as a substitute English teacher.

Her friends, Lois and Eleanor, were cheerful, friendly souls who admired Jessica and were, if truth were told, a little in awe of her. If their intelligence did not quite match up to hers, she at least never gave any indication of being aware of the fact.

Following their return from the theatre, the three ladies were drinking coffee in Jessica's home, a large Victorian house on a pleasant, tree-lined block in the small coastal town of Cabot Cove, Maine. In spite of many invitations from numerous relatives throughout the country for her to make her home with them, Jessica had lived alone since the death of her husband some years before. The house was too big for her, she knew. And every corner of it evoked poignant memories. But she did love the house, and the town, and by keeping every minute of her days occupied she was managing—now, at last—to hold the ache at bay.

"Say, Jessica." Eleanor put down her coffee cup suddenly. "Why don't you write a mystery?"

"Now that's an idea!" exclaimed Lois. "After all, you're a teacher of English, so you know all about literature and grammar and stuff."

Jessica gazed at them silently for a few seconds. Then she smiled. "Funny you should say that, girls."

For a moment they looked blank. Then Eleanor gave a squeal. "Jess—you mean you *have?*"

Jessica shrugged. "Well, sort of."

"My, how thrilling!" Lois' eyes were big. "Oh, Jess, you must let us read it."

"Certainly not," Jessica said firmly.

"But why?"

"Because it's simply not good enough."

"Oh, Jessica, nonsense! I'm sure it's just wonderful!"

"You can't possibly say that, Eleanor. You know nothing about the story."

"But we know *you,*" said Lois.

"You're sweet, girls, but I know *it.* In addition to writing it, I've read it. Which I think a lot of authors fail to do."

"At least tell us what it's called," said Eleanor.

"You'll laugh."

"No, we won't, honestly. Will we, Lois?"

"Cross our hearts."

"Well, it's called *The Corpse Danced at Midnight.* Just an old-fashioned whodunit."

"Oo." Lois gave a wriggle. "Thrilling!"

"Is it a *real* corpse? And does it *really* dance?"

"Eleanor, a real corpse could hardly *really* dance." Lois laughed. "It's not a horror story."

"No, I suppose not," Eleanor admitted. "But, Jess, you mean you're not going to try and get it published?"

"No way, my dear."

"Oh, Jess, I think you're so stupid. It might be a best seller."

Jessica laughed. "Not a chance, Eleanor."

"Oh, do let us read it," Lois pleaded. "Or just the first couple of chapters. We'll tell you exactly what we think. Honestly. Won't we, Eleanor?"

"Cross our hearts."

Jessica hesitated. She was too kind to say it, but their opinion of her book would be quite valueless to her. She was very fond of Lois and Eleanor. But they were to literary criticism what John Wayne had been to ballet dancing.

She gave a sigh. Oh well, perhaps it wouldn't do any harm to let them read the first two chapters. At least, if they didn't like it (and whatever they *said*, she'd know what they *thought*), it would tell her clearly that the book was even worse than she suspected.

"All right," she said. "You win." She got to her feet.

"Oh, thanks, Jess."

"Have you got two copies?" Eleanor asked eagerly.

"Afraid not. You'll have to take turns. Toss a coin, or something." She picked up her purse, rummaged in it, and drew out a small key.

"Isn't that a bit risky?" Eleanor said. "Not having a second copy, I mean."

"Not at all—as I don't intend to send it away. I have my original manuscript, of course."

Jessica crossed to a large, old-fashioned dark wood bureau in the corner of the room and unlocked one of the doors. She opened it, reached inside, and then stood quite still. She bent down, peered into the cupboard, and started groping with both hands.

"What's the matter, Jess?" Eleanor spoke sharply.

Jessica slowly straightened up and turned to her friends. Her face was blank. "It's gone," she said. "The typescript of my book. Someone must have stolen it."

Fifteen minutes later Jessica sank back down into her chair. "Well," she said slowly, "there's certainly nothing else missing. That's one relief."

"You've checked in every room?" Lois queried.

Jessica nodded.

Eleanor was looking mystified. "But who on earth would break in and just steal a manuscript?"

Suddenly Lois' face lit up. "Another author, of course!" she said triumphantly. "He wants to steal your plot."

"Lois, until twenty minutes ago nobody in the world but myself knew the book existed."

Lois' face fell. "Oh."

"Hadn't you better call the police?" Eleanor asked.

"No."

"But Jessica, why not?"

"Because I know who's taken it. It just this moment hit me. It could only be one person."

In Grady Fletcher's Greenwich Village apartment the phone rang. Grady answered it. He was an eager, fresh-faced young man of twenty-seven, tall, slim, and nearly always smiling. Basically a romantic and idealist, his chosen profession of accounting forced him, perhaps fortunately, to bank down his natural exuberance. But it could do little to quench his considerable charm.

"Hullo?" he said.

He heard a familiar voice. "Grady?"

"Oh, hi, Aunt Jess. How are you?"

"Very well. Grady, I'll come straight to the point. Did you take the typescript of a novel with you last month when you left here?"

"Oh."

"I take it that means yes?"

"How did you guess it was me?"

"It couldn't have been anyone else. It had to be somebody staying in the house, not an ordinary thief. Grady, why did you do it?"

"I wanted to read it."

"Why didn't you ask?"

"I thought you'd say no. You remember, when I was staying with you, I came in one day just as you were putting the manuscript away?"

11

"Ah, I thought you caught a glimpse of it."

"I did. And for a moment you looked kind of embarrassed. I was intrigued—though I soon guessed those papers were a novel. I just had to read it. But knowing you, I was sure you wouldn't think it good enough to let anyone see it. So I realized I'd have to sneak it. Trouble was, you always kept the bureau locked. Until, that is, the very last day of my visit. You'd been to the bureau for something else and you left the key in. So when you went out of the room I grabbed the novel and slipped it in my case. I felt a bit awful at first. But after all, you *have* always told me to treat the house completely as my own, so . . ."

"Oh, don't be silly! I don't mind *that*. But all the same, it was very naughty of you to take the manuscript away."

Grady grinned. "You're the only person in the world who ever calls me naughty."

"More's the pity, probably. I could be very angry, Grady."

"Oh no, you couldn't, Aunt Jess—not with me. You know I'm your favorite relative."

"I know you're very conceited."

"Not at all. Just honest. Come on, now; it's true, isn't it?"

"Grady!"

"Will it help if I tell you it's mutual?"

"Flattery . . ."

"I know: is the sincerest form of imitation." The young man paused. "Hang on, there's something wrong there."

"Grady, you're . . ."

"Incorrigible?"

"I was going to say impossible."

"I like incorrigible better."

"This has gone on quite long enough," Jessica said firmly.

"Okay. Goodbye, Aunt Jess."

"Grady, don't hang up."

"Only kidding. Aunt Jess, I'm extremely sorry if I've upset you. I shouldn't have done it."

"Very well. We'll say no more about it—provided you return the manuscript at once. You have finished reading it, I suppose?"

"I have."

There was a pause. Then: "I see," said Jessica.

There was a longer pause. "You still there, Aunt Jess?"

"Er, yes."

"Something else you wanted to say?"

Jessica sighed. "You're waiting for me to ask how you liked it, aren't you?"

"If you really want to know . . ."

"All right, you'd better tell me."

Grady cleared his throat. "Well, to be absolutely frank . . ." He broke off, then laughed. "Aunt Jess, I think it's great."

"Really, Grady?"

"I couldn't put it down. I stayed up till three one morning finishing it."

"Well, that's very gratifying. Thank you. I value your opinion very much, Grady. But as you've finished it, I would like you to send it back now."

Grady sighed. "Afraid I can't do that. I loaned it to a friend."

"Oh, Grady, really!"

"It was so good, I just had to tell someone. And then this person naturally wanted to read it."

13

"Then ask for it back at once. If he hasn't finished it, you can *tell* him the end—if he's interested."

"It's a she, actually."

"Tell *her* the end, then."

"Oh, she's finished it."

"Then what *is* the problem?"

"Well, as a matter of fact, she's passed it on to her boss."

"Her boss? But why . . . I mean, who . . . ?"

"His name's Preston Giles."

"I don't care what his name is," Jessica said irritably. "I'm only interested in . . ." She broke off. "Preston Giles? That name seems to ring a bell."

"It should—for anyone interested in books. He's head of Coventry House."

"Coventry House? The publishers?"

"That's right. Now get hold of yourself, Aunt Jess, and listen. Kitt—oh, that's her name: Kitt Donovan—thought her firm might be interested in the book. Of course, Kitt doesn't pick books for publication herself; she's in the publicity department. So she took it straight to Mr. Giles. It's a terrific break. I mean, normally books have to go through the whole mill—readers, editors. But Giles promised Kitt that he would read *Corpse* personally."

"Read *what* personally?"

"*Corpse.* Oh, that's what Kitt and I have been calling it—sort of shorthand, you know. Where was I? Oh yes, he's promised to read it personally. Of course, he's very busy, so we don't know whether he's actually started it yet. Naturally she can't keep on pestering him about . . ."

"Grady, I'm not a writer. I've been filling in time since your uncle died. I wrote it to help keep my mind occupied, and as a sort of challenge—just to see if I could do it. I did think that if one day I wrote a book I could be proud of, I might send it to a publisher. But not this one. I want your friend to get it back.''

Grady gave a groan. ''I couldn't ask her to do that. Not after Giles agreed to read it personally. I couldn't do that to Kitt. It'd make her look a fool.''

''But surely, when she explains that I simply don't want the book published . . .''

''That's just it. Giles doesn't know Kitt didn't have the author's permission to submit it. And *she* doesn't know, either. She thinks I have yours. She'd be terribly sore with me if she found out I didn't. And I'd hate to get Kitt sore with me. Oh, Aunt Jess, she's a wonderful girl.''

''I'm sure she is, Grady. They always are.''

''Oh, but she's different. She . . .''

''Her difference is not the point at issue.'' Jessica sighed. ''Oh, I don't know. I suppose I'll *have* to leave the book with him now.''

''That's great. I just knew you'd agree.''

''Which is more than I knew. How long do you think before . . . ?''

''Oh, not more than a few weeks, I'm sure. We'll just have to hope Giles doesn't like it.''

''I don't think I'd go that far. I'd like him to *like* it. That doesn't mean I have to let him publish it, does it?''

''No, I guess not. Okay, Aunt Jess, I'll get back to you the moment I hear anything.''

''Grady, one more thing: this girl—Kitt—is it serious this time?''

Grady didn't answer for a moment. ''Yes, it is. At least, it is with me.''

''Good. I suggest you find out if it is with her. It's as well to have these matters quite clear. Goodbye, Grady.''

''Goodbye, Aunt Jess.''

Chapter Two

FOR the next week or so Jessica's life proceeded on its usual busy but fairly unexciting course. She continued her work as substitute English teacher at Cabot Cove High School; she was active in the PTA; she bicycled and jogged and ran her house; she went out to eat with Lois and Eleanor.

But she didn't do any more writing.

It was ten days before Grady returned her call.

"Aunt Jess," he said when they'd exchanged greetings, "the news about *Corpse* is good and bad. Which do you want first?"

"The good."

"Well, Preston Giles enjoyed it very much and he'll be writing to tell you so."

"Oh, how nice," Jessica said. "I'll look forward to his letter. And I suppose the bad news is that nonetheless he doesn't want to publish it? But that's not bad news, Grady. I meant what I said: I don't *want* it published. So really . . ."

"You've got it wrong, Aunt Jessica. He does want to publish it. The bad news is that you're going to have quite a fight on your hands to stop him."

Jessica gave a gasp. "I don't believe it! He must be out of his mind."

"Not obviously so."

"You told him no, of course."

"I've told him nothing. I haven't seen him. He just today informed Kitt they were going to offer you a contract."

"Grady, you must . . ."

"It's out of my hands, Aunt Jess. You'll have to tell them yourself. Sorry and all that. Look, I must go: the Captain's just called a staff meeting. But congratulations—or commiserations. I don't know which. Bye."

He hung up.

Jessica had genuinely intended to say no to Preston Giles. But the next day his letter arrived. It was very charming. And the advance he was offering—really, it was extremely generous. It would come in most useful. And, after all, she told herself, if Grady and Kitt Donovan *and* Mr. Giles all liked the book—well, she supposed it couldn't be too bad. Finally she succumbed and signed the contracts.

After that, rather surprisingly, nothing happened for a long time. Then one day, out of the blue, the proofs arrived. Jessica spent hours laboriously going over them for errors, and unnecessarily rechecking the spelling of dozens of words that in reality she knew perfectly how to spell.

A few months later the dust jacket turned up in the mail. To Jessica's relief it was in excellent taste, not at all like the lurid covers on some crime novels. In passing, it occurred to her that tasteful covers didn't necessarily help sales. But then, she reasoned, just because someone was publishing her book didn't mean that anyone would bother to read it. Every year hundreds of books died quietly and quickly, never to be heard of again.

She just hoped that Coventry House didn't actually lose money on it, that was all. . . .

Jessica stood outside the Cabot Cove Bookstore and stared disbelievingly at the window display. Copies of *The Corpse Danced at Midnight* by J. B. Fletcher filled all available space, while a huge, almost life-size picture of Jessica herself towered over them. Jessica squirmed inwardly. In the very center of the window was a placard that carried a photostat of the National Literary Circle best seller list. The eighth book, circled in red, was Jessica's. At the top of the placard was the legend in large type: NUMBER EIGHT BEST SELLER.

Jessica turned to see two of her students, a boy and a girl, standing beside her. She blushed slightly. They grinned at her.

"It's great, Mrs. Fletcher," said the boy.

The girl added: "Just terrific."

"Oh, thank you, Gail, Joe. But really, there must be some mistake."

At that moment the curtain at the rear of the window was pulled aside and the store owner appeared. He reached forward and removed the placard.

"There!" Jessica again swung around on the youngsters. "Didn't I tell you?" she asked triumphantly. "It *was* a mistake. All this fuss! I knew it didn't amount to anything."

But as she was speaking the bookseller reappeared. In his hand was a new placard. It read: THIS WEEK!! NUMBER TWO BEST SELLER.

Jessica looked utterly dismayed. "Oh dear," she sighed.

* * *

Kitt Donovan stood in the reception area of McCallum Enterprises Inc. in New York City and critically surveyed a man's picture.

Kitt was a smart, strikingly attractive girl of twenty-four. If not actually beautiful, she had a freshness and vivacity that more than made up for it. Several years of working in the sophisticated world of New York publishing had done nothing to kill an innocence, spontaneity, and kindheartedness that were as refreshing as a spring day. She was very much in love with Grady Fletcher and he with her.

It was not, however, Grady's photograph that Kitt was studying at the moment, but a promotional poster advertising Cap'n Caleb's Chowder Houses. It had much the effect on her that the placard in the bookstore had had on Jessica.

The poster featured the face of Cap'n Caleb McCallum, a robust man in his early fifties, with white hair and flinty gray eyes. He was holding a bowl of chowder, and underneath was the slogan: OVER A BILLION BOWLS SOLD!

"Kitt, what a great surprise!"

She turned to see Grady Fletcher approaching from the direction of the elevator. He was conservatively dressed in a dark three-piece suit and looked every inch a successful CPA, which he wasn't—not just yet.

He took Kitt's hand. "I didn't expect to see you today."

"I know. But something's come up."

"About *Corpse?* To do with Aunt Jess?"

"Yes."

"Something bad?"

"She may think so. Though actually far from it."

"I don't follow."

"Patience. Look, can you manage lunch?"

"You bet." Grady told the receptionist he would return at two o'clock. Then he took Kitt by her arm. "Let's go."

As they were crossing the lobby, Kitt nodded toward the big poster. "Is that true?"

"What? Oh, the billion-bowls bit. I've no idea."

"I thought you were supposed to be his accountant."

They passed into the street. "One very lowly, fledgling member of his army of accountants," Grady said. "And with three new Chowder Houses opening every week somewhere in the country—to the horror of gourmets everywhere—he needs every one of us. Where do you want to eat?"

"Isn't there a Chowder House near here?" Kitt asked innocently.

Grady shuddered. "Thankfully, there's nothing in my contract of employment that says I have to eat the lousy stuff. Come on, I know a great little French restaurant just around the corner."

They started to walk. "What's he a captain of?" Kitt asked.

"Who—Caleb? Industry, I suppose. Certainly not of any known ship. Though now I come to think of it, he did buy himself a yacht recently—called, believe it or not, *Chowder King*. But he was calling himself Cap'n long ago. You know, I wouldn't object to Captain half as much."

"What's he like?"

"Well, as somebody said the other day, he's a man finely attuned to the product he sells: cold fish."

"Let's give the Cap'n his due," Kitt said. "If he and my boss weren't friends, you and I would never have met."

"Great thing, friendship," said Grady.

They entered the restaurant, ordered food and wine, then sat back and looked at each other with satisfaction.

"Now," Grady said, "what's all this about my revered aunt?"

"Do you think she'd come to New York for a week or so?"

"She might. What for?"

"Oh, just to autograph her book in a major Fifth Avenue store, be interviewed on the radio and by the press, and appear on several TV programs. Including the *Today* show."

Grady stared at her. "All that? You're not serious!"

She nodded.

"I can't believe it! *Your* doing?"

"Well . . ." She gave a little shrug and pursed her lips.

"Clever girl!"

"No, actually, I haven't had to hype her much at all. I mean, *Corpse* is at number two. Could go to the top. A first novel by a middle-aged widow lady in Maine! It makes your aunt of interest to a lot of people. Question is: will she play ball?"

"You leave her to me," Grady said. "Come back to the office with me after lunch and I'll call her—personal charge, of course. Can't have company accountants setting a bad example."

Back at MacCallum Enterprises an hour later, Grady and Kitt were waiting for an elevator. One arrived. The doors opened and a beautiful young woman emerged. She had jet-black hair, was immaculately turned out, and wore a dress that made Kitt's mouth water.

The young woman smiled intimately as she passed them. "Hullo, Grady," she murmured in a low and seductive voice. Then she was gone, leaving behind her the subtle aroma of expensive perfume.

Grady, looking embarrassed, replied, "Oh, er, good afternoon, er, Ashley," to her swayingly retreating back. He then ushered Kitt into the empty elevator. The doors closed and Grady pressed a button.

Kitt was round-eyed. *"Who* was that?"

"The girl? Oh, her name's Ashley Vickers."

"That outfit—oh boy! And what looks!"

"Oh, you think she's pretty?" Grady said casually.

In answer, Kitt kicked him sharply on the shin.

He gave a muted yell. "What's that for?"

"You know quite well. Pretending you've hardly noticed her!" She mimicked: *"Oh, you think she's pretty?* She's absolutely stunning, and you know it. What's she do here, anyway?"

"She's Caleb's personal assistant."

Kitt's eyebrows went up. "Real-ly?" she said slowly.

"Now, honey, don't get any ideas."

"You're telling *me* not to get ideas? You think the Cap'n hasn't had a few?"

"Whatever ideas he's had, there's not an iota of evidence he's put them into practice."

"Want to bet? You don't buy dresses like that on a PA's salary. There is a *Mrs.* McCallum, isn't there?"

"Yes, but"—he lowered his voice—"not another word. I've long suspected these elevators are bugged."

The elevator stopped and the doors opened. "Come on, let's call Aunt Jess."

"No, Grady, I can't," said Jessica.

"But it's all arranged. They've booked you on all these shows."

"They shouldn't have done so without my permission."

"But these publicity junkets come with the territory."

"What would I say on television? I'd make a fool of myself."

"Nonsense. They'll love you. Oh, come on, Aunt Jess, how about it?"

Jessica hesitated. She was facing an alarming prospect. But it *would* be an experience—not the sort of thing you ought to back away from just because you were scared of making a fool of yourself.

"Well," she said doubtfully, "I suppose I could come for a day or two."

"Terrific. Can you be here Monday? Around midday?"

"Well . . . yes."

"Okay. Let me know what time your train's arriving and I'll meet you at Grand Central. Must go. See you Monday." He hung up.

Jessica put the receiver down slowly and turned to confront the openmouthed stares of Lois and Eleanor, who had been listening to her end of the conversation.

"Jessica," Eleanor asked excitedly, "are you really going to be on television?"

"I'm afraid I am."

Lois studied her critically from head to foot. Then she shook her head disapprovingly. "Not like *that*, you're not."

Jessica looked down at herself. She was wearing a tweed suit, with a white sweater and sensible shoes.

"Why, what's the matter?"

"Jessica, millions of people are going to be watching you. You have to look, er, *now—with it.*"

"*Au courant,*" said Eleanor smoothly.

"And those tweeds have got to go," said Lois.

The next day was one of the most miserable of Jessica's life. Eleanor and Lois took her on a round of local dress shops and boutiques, virtually forcing her to try on dozens of outfits, all of which, she was assured, reflected the latest

big-city trends. Eventually, her resistance worn down, she
found herself paying out good money for several positively
bizarre creations, including one outlandish tentlike dress in
gaudy red and white stripes, which she felt she ought to be
saluting rather than wearing. But anything, Jessica thought,
to get her two friends off her back.

However, the ordeal was far from over. Next it was to a
beauty parlor, where the face was smeared with mud and her
body pounded and pressed unmercifully and interminably.

Finally, her hair was shampooed, blown dry, brushed,
and twisted. She left eventually, her head topped with a
strange coiffure that the hairdresser promised was the latest
rage in New York, and which Lois and Eleanor assured her
did wonders for her.

By the end of the day Jessica was exhausted. As she staggered into her house and flopped onto a chair, she told herself that New York couldn't possibly be worse than this.

Jessica alighted from the train and the conductor handed
down her one modest suitcase.

"Thank you, Daniel. Thanks for all your help." She
fumbled in her purse for a dollar and held it out.

"Oh no, ma'am." He declined it firmly. "It's been my
pleasure."

"Are you sure? Well, as you wish. Goodbye—and I do
hope your boy gets that scholarship."

"Thank you, Mrs. Fletcher. You going to be all right
now?"

"Oh yes. My nephew's meeting me." She turned. "Ah,
there he is."

"Then have a nice stay, ma'am."

He tipped his cap and moved back into the train as

Grady, followed by Kitt, came hurrying along the platform. Jessica put down her case and lifted her arms to Grady.

"Aunt Jess!" He gave her a hug. "It's great to see you."

"And you, my boy. Grady, I'm sorry if you don't like the way I'm dressed and how my hair is done, but nature never intended me to look like a barber pole or a kitchen mop."

He held her at arm's length and regarded her intently. "I don't know what you mean. You look just fine. Exactly the same as always."

"That's what I mean. I was very nearly modernized, but at the last moment I rebelled, so New York will have to take me as I am."

"That's all we want. Oh, Aunt Jess, this is Kitt Donovan."

Jessica smiled. "So you're the young lady I have to thank for all this."

"Guilty," said Kitt, with a grin.

"Nevertheless, I'm delighted to meet you." Jessica held out her hand.

"It's mutual, Mrs. Fletcher. Grady's told me so much about you."

"Well, he hasn't told me nearly enough about you, my dear. Only that you're wonderful and different."

"Quiet, please, Aunt Jess," Grady hissed. "You'll be giving her a swollen head. Now, let's not stand around here any longer." He picked up her case. "Where's the rest of your luggage?"

"That's all there is."

"Gee, you do travel light."

"Where's the first stop?" Jessica asked.

"Coventry House, if that's all right with you," Kitt told her. "Mr. Giles is looking forward to meeting you. Unless you'd like to check into your hotel first?"

Jessica shook her head. "By no means. Lead on to Coventry House. I'm very much looking forward to meeting Mr. Giles."

Preston Giles clasped Jessica warmly by the hand. "My dear Mrs. Fletcher, welcome to Manhattan. And to Coventry House. We're all delighted about *The Corpse Danced at Midnight*. It's going splendidly."

"Thank you," said Jessica, "it's very exciting for me."

"I do hope you're quite happy with the way everything's been handled?"

Jessica eyed him keenly, summing him up. He was a distinguished-looking man with a strong, rather handsome face, thick hair graying at the temples, and very deep-set eyes. She put his age at somewhere in the late fifties. He didn't look altogether well, being rather pale and having dark circles under his eyes. But his handshake was firm.

A workaholic, she decided. She had made a few inquiries and discovered that Coventry House was very much a one-man creation. Preston Giles had taken over a small rundown publishing house and, with a seemingly unerring instinct for popular taste, had produced a stream of best-selling books.

Now he gave a surreptitious glance at the clock on the wall of his office. Jessica got the impression that, for all his courtesy, he didn't really want to listen to her replies. His words appeared automatic, as though they'd been spoken many times before. He seemed under some pressure. He'd be relieved, she felt, to be done with her quickly. And she determined not to let *him* dismiss *her*.

She murmured that everything had been quite satisfactory.

"Fine, fine. And I'm sure I can leave you safely in Kitt's

capable hands. I'm absolutely up to my ears in work or I'd be delighted to escort you myself. But I've had a dozen crises already this morning.''

"Well, I certainly don't want to be number thirteen," Jessica remarked.

He smiled absently. "We must have dinner while you're in town and really get acquainted . . ."

"Do you eat apples?" Jessica interrupted.

"I beg your pardon?" He stared. For the first time she had his full attention.

"Apples. You really should, you know. The pectin. It's good for the complexion. You seem, if I may say so, very gray."

"Actually, I haven't been sleeping well . . ."

"Apples," said Jessica for the third time.

He gave a weak smile. "Yes. Thank you."

"And now," she said firmly, "you really must excuse me, Mr. Giles. I understand there are several engagements scheduled today, and I haven't even checked into my hotel yet. Goodbye for now."

She smiled demurely, and a moment later was outside.

"Well, that was short and sweet," said Grady, as they walked along the corridor.

Jessica nodded. "He was very charming. But definitely distrait."

Kitt said awkwardly, "I'm awfully sorry, Mrs. Fletcher. I'm sure if he were less busy . . ."

"Kitt, I'm certain it's far better to have a publisher who's too busy than one who doesn't have enough to do. Now I think perhaps you'd better take me to my hotel. I must prepare myself to meet the inquisitors."

* * *

The next few days were undoubtedly the most hectic that Jessica had ever spent. A harassed Kitt rushed her from one engagement to another.

There were not one, but two lengthy and tiring autographing sessions, at which most of the customers required long and involved inscriptions—or dedications to unknown people with names like Booboo, Attila, Big Chief, or Snuggles. One man purchased eight copies and, to Jessica's relief, demanded only her signature and the date on each.

"My, you must be a real book lover," she said as she started signing.

"Never open one. These are just an investment. If you turn out to be somebody, maybe they'll be worth somethin'. It's a long shot, though, I guess," he added as he staggered away under his load.

Jessica didn't know whether to laugh or cry.

She appeared on four TV shows. One interviewer was a supercilious highbrow critic who plainly regarded most detective fiction with contempt and used the occasion as a chance to air his views on Literature; another moderator was a severe and opinionated young woman who had convinced herself that *Corpse* was in fact a feminist tract and tried by every means at her disposal—though unsuccessfully—to make Jessica admit this. (She also, to Jessica's intense chagrin, gave away the identity of the murderer.)

Jessica appeared next in a discussion program—broadcast live at one a.m.—with three other writers, all experienced TV performers, who expatiated at inordinate length about authors and books she had never heard of. She hardly got a word in edgeways.

She was grilled by an abrasive and semiliterate radio talk show host who called her Jennifer and only seemed interested in finding out if she *(a)* was living in sin with anyone or *(b)* had a criminal record.

She was interviewed by three press reporters—one bored, one incredibly young and horribly nervous, and one drunk.

In four days she was asked about her favorite food, color, breed of dog; her star sign; and her opinion on capital punishment, drug abuse, environmental pollution, gun control, smoking, UFOs, the Olympic Games, and whole-grain bread. Nobody listened to her answers. Nobody asked her questions she'd prepared herself to answer: what were the most important qualities of a detective story? who were her favorite mystery writers? who had influenced her? and so on. None of her inquisitors, in fact, seemed very interested in mystery stories. And certainly none of them had read her book through from beginning to end.

Jessica also attended two cocktail parties and was joint guest of honor at a literary luncheon with an avant-garde Turkish poet who gave a forty-minute speech in his native language, which had to be translated sentence by sentence by someone who seemed fluent in neither English nor Turkish. Moreover, the food was horrible.

During all this time she saw hardly anything of Grady, wasn't able to catch any Broadway shows, see any sights, or do any shopping. And there was no word of any kind from Preston Giles. Kitt alone, always by her side and always cheerful, made everything just bearable.

Nevertheless, when Jessica was lying in bed on Thursday night, trying to decide which was aching worse, her feet or her head, she came to a firm decision.

First thing the next morning she tore into small fragments the list of engagements for the day, which Kitt had left with her the previous evening, and dropped them in the wastebasket. Then she phoned Coventry House.

"Miss Donovan, please," she said when the receptionist answered.

"I'm sorry, she's not in yet."

"Then will you please give her a message? You'd better take this down. Ready?"

"Yes, ma'am."

"This is Jessica Fletcher. Tell Miss Donovan I thank her for all her great personal kindnesses, and I hope she'll come visit with me at Cabot Cove one day soon. Got that?"

". . . one day soon. Yes, Mrs. Fletcher."

"And please tell her to cancel all my future engagements in New York. I'm going home today. All right?"

"Yes, but Mrs. Fletcher . . . ma'am . . . I really don't . . ."

"Thank you so much. Goodbye."

And with a sigh of relief Jessica hung up.

Jessica walked happily along the train platform, carrying her suitcase. She felt carefree for the first time in nearly a week. She was going home.

Then suddenly she heard a voice calling behind her.

"Aunt Jess—wait!"

She turned to see Grady sprinting along the platform toward her. A few yards behind him was Kitt. Jessica gave a sigh of resignation and put down her suitcase. "I might have guessed," she murmured to herself.

"Thank heavens we caught you," Grady gasped. "Why didn't you phone me before you left?"

"Well, it doesn't seem to have mattered, does it? Kitt obviously did. I'm sorry, Grady. I didn't realize you'd want so much to see me off."

"I don't want to see you off. I want you to stay."

"Why?"

"For one thing, I've barely set eyes on you since you've been here."

"That's hardly my fault, Grady."

"Nor mine."

"Quite true. But I think in the future it'll be much more satisfactory if we get together only in Cabot Cove. Now, honestly, don't you agree?"

Pleadingly, Kitt said: "Oh, Mrs. Fletcher, please don't go yet. I have several more things arranged with media people. They'll be mad with Coventry House if you don't show, and Mr. Giles will blame me."

"Kitt, my dear, he won't be able to. I shall write to him, praising you to the skies and telling him that *nobody* could have stopped me from leaving. Four days in the Big Apple have been quite enough for me, thank you."

Grady cleared his throat. "I think you can tell him now to his face, Aunt Jess." He jerked his head.

Jessica looked along the platform and saw Preston Giles hurrying toward them. In his hands was a big bunch of long-stemmed red roses. He came up and, almost diffidently, handed them to her.

"Mrs. Fletcher," he said quietly. "I'm mortified by my behavior. I've come to beg your forgiveness."

"Mr. Giles," said Jessica, "I'm sure you're a charming man, but for several days I have been insulted, browbeaten, and patronized, and I say no, thank you. Back in Cabot Cove the only things with claws are the lobsters. And we eat them."

"I know how you feel, believe me," he said. "It took me years to get used to this town."

He smiled gently. "Look, I'm having a few houseguests at my place in the country this weekend. And tomorrow night I'm throwing quite a big party. I'd like you to join

31

me.'' He looked at Kitt and Grady. ''All of you,'' he added. He turned back to Jessica. ''You'll meet some real people— not critics and columnists, but my friends. Drive up with me tomorrow morning. And then on Monday, if you still want to go back home, I'll put you on this train personally. Fair enough?''

Jessica looked down at the flowers, then back up at him. ''We'd better get these in water,'' she said, ''before they wilt.''

Chapter Three

THE big Mercedes sedan sped along the elm-lined country road in upstate New York and whipped around a bend. Behind the wheel, Preston Giles looked more relaxed than Jessica had yet seen him.

"I suppose we get used to these self-important media types," he was saying. "We live with them because we have to."

"Why do you have to?" Jessica asked.

"Why? Well, because we . . . ." He broke off and chuckled. "You know, I'm not sure I know why. I'll tell you something, though, Mrs. J. B. Fletcher: you could become a very disruptive influence in my life."

"Mr. Giles, only my students call me Mrs. Fletcher."

"And Mr. Giles is that stuffed shirt in the three-piece suit I left back in Manhattan."

They smiled at each other.

"I don't know about you, Jessica," Preston said, "but I'm glad we let your nephew and Kitt find their own way out here."

A few minutes later the car passed an old-fashioned road sign, which carried the words: ENTERING NEW HOL-VANG. DRIVE CAREFULLY.

"Oh, are we there?" Jessica asked.

"Just about."

Preston braked and turned off the road into a long drive-way. They swept along it, to pull up eventually in front of an enormous and very attractive house.

Jessica looked around her. "My, isn't it all lovely!"

"Well, I like it here."

A butler had emerged from the house, and he opened the passenger door for Jessica to alight.

"Good afternoon, madam."

"Good afternoon." She got out. "Thank you."

Preston came around from the driver's side. "Davis, this is Mrs. Fletcher. Is her room ready?"

"Yes, sir."

"Fine. Her luggage is in the trunk."

Preston took Jessica's arm and they went through the front door into a large, elegantly furnished foyer.

"This is delightful, Preston," Jessica said with genuine admiration.

"Thank you. I hope you'll make yourself completely at home. Now, would you care for a drink, some tea . . . ?"

"Not just yet. I'd prefer to go straight to my room and freshen up, if I may."

Jessica found she had been allocated an airy, beautifully proportioned room overlooking the swimming pool. Davis put down her luggage.

"Will there be anything more, madam?"

"No, thank you."

He turned to leave. "I shall send a maid to unpack and as-sist you."

"Oh, mercy, no!" Jessica said hastily. "I've done my own packing and unpacking for a good few years."

"Just as you wish, madam." He made for the door.

"You know something, Davis?"

He turned back. "What, madam?"

Jessica surveyed him thoughtfully. "I don't think I've ever seen a real live butler before."

"Indeed, madam?"

"Indeed. I've seen them in the movies—though they're only actors, of course. I've read about butlers; I've even written about one. But until now I've never met one."

"We are a dying breed, madam."

"Oh, I do hope not. Rare perhaps, endangered maybe. But not dying."

He smiled. "Thank you, Mrs. Fletcher."

"Well, I just wanted to say that if you see me watching you closely over the weekend, please don't take it amiss. It'll just be research. *My* butler was based too much on *other* writers' butlers. I want my next one to be grounded in real life."

"I'll be honored to be a model, madam. But may I ask: will your next story be one in which the butler did it?"

"Wait and see, Davis; wait and see."

Jessica had taken time before leaving the city to buy some new clothes. She had just finished changing into a casual outfit and was seated at the dressing table fixing her face, when there was a tap on her door.

It was Grady.

"Hullo, dear," she said. "Sit down. Where's Kitt?"

"Taking a shower." He perched on the edge of her bed. "Well, what do you think of everything?" he asked.

"Very impressive. I had no idea Preston lived in such style."

"Oh, it's Preston now, is it?"

"Why not?"

"No reason at all. I'm delighted you've been reconciled to everything and you've stopped talking of running back to Cabot Cove."

"I still could. I'm far from sure the high life is for me. But tell me, Grady, about this weekend. Who's going to be here, exactly? Do you know?"

"Not really. But I just caught a glimpse of my revered boss—and his wife."

"Captain McCallum?"

"Yep. Giles is an old friend of them both."

"I see. It'll be interesting to meet your boss at last."

"You have a treat in store, Aunt Jess," he said sardonically.

"You know, Grady, he ought to do something about the food he serves at those Chowder Houses. I took the girls to one a while back—just out of loyalty to you, really—and honestly, it wasn't very good."

"I'm just an accountant, Aunt Jess, not the cook."

"But there are so many little ways in which things could be made better, at very little extra cost . . ."

"Well, you'll have plenty of opportunity to suggest them to him yourself. But if you're talking about extra cost, you can forget it."

"You don't make him sound very nice, Grady. He looks so cheerful on those posters."

"I figure it was an effort for him to hold that grin for the one-hundredth of a second it took to snap the picture."

"Don't you think you might be a little prejudiced, Grady?"

"Perhaps. I only see him at the office. There, he's a . . . well, a *driven* man. Maybe socially he's a different character." He stood up. "Ready to go down?"

Jessica picked up her purse and checked its contents. "You say Mrs. McCallum is here? What's she like?"

"Louise? I've never spoken to her. Seems a bit sour— hardly surprisingly. They say she hits the bottle more than she should."

"Oh, how sad."

"Well, at least she can afford it." He opened the door. "Come along, Aunt Jess, and judge them yourself—as you will do anyway, whatever I say."

They went downstairs. On the terrace they found Preston seated, sipping long, cool drinks with an attractive woman in her mid-forties.

Preston stood up as they approached. "Jessica, you look charming." He introduced Louise McCallum.

Louise held out her hand. "I'm delighted to know you, Mrs. Fletcher. I just loved your book."

"Why, thank you," Jessica said.

Preston continued the introductions. "Louise, I expect you know Grady Fletcher, Jessica's nephew."

"Well, we've never been formally introduced," Louise said. "Though I've seen you at the office, Mr. Fletcher, of course. Caleb talks of you as one of his most promising young men."

Grady look amazed—and a little embarrassed. "That's very kind of him. I thought he'd hardly noticed me."

"Oh, he's noticed you."

Jessica smiled to herself. "Where *is* the Captain?" she asked.

Louise jerked her head. "You can hear him."

Jessica had been vaguely conscious for some time of gun-shots coming from an area out of sight at the other side of the pool.

"Oh, is that Captain McCallum?"

"That's Caleb, all right," Louise said dryly. "Terminating skeets with extreme prejudice."

"Is he a keen marksman?" Jessica inquired politely.

"I think he just likes smashing things," said Louise.

Grady gave a muffled snort and hastily turned it into a cough. Fortunately, at that moment Kitt, looking fresh and cool, emerged from the house. Preston introduced her to Louise.

Just as they were shaking hands, the air was suddenly shattered by a gigantic bang.

Everyone gave a start and most of those present instinctively, but far too late, raised their hands to their ears.

"What was *that?*" Jessica asked a little shakily.

"Sonic boom, I'm afraid," Preston said in an apologetic tone. "We've got an airport down the road. One of the few drawbacks about this place."

"What with that and my husband," said Louise, "we're not likely to have a very peaceful weekend."

"Actually, I think he's stopped," said Preston.

Sure enough, the gun seemed to have fallen silent, and a few seconds later they saw Caleb McCallum approaching. There was a shotgun crooked in his arm, and accompanying him was a beautiful young woman.

As the pair got closer, Kitt drew her breath in sharply and dug Grady in the ribs. McCallum's companion was Ashley Vickers.

As they approached, and before anyone else could speak, Louise called in a bright voice: "Good shooting, darling."

"How would you know?" he asked shortly.

"I could hear the skeets shattering from here. Besides, I'm sure the presence of Miss Vickers always spurs you to the peak of performance—whatever you're doing. Tell me, Miss Vickers, did you try your hand?"

Ashley gave a tight-lipped smile. "Oh no, I'm hopeless with guns."

"Never mind, dear. We can't all be good at *everything.*"

"Why don't you come and give it a try, Louise?" her husband asked. Then he added pointedly: "All it requires is a clear eye and a steady hand."

"I don't think so, Caleb, thanks. I might miss the skeet and hit a person. And the steadier my hand, the more likely I'd be to do it."

Preston hurriedly performed general introductions.

After McCallum and Ashley had been presented to Jessica and Kitt, Davis arrived, apparently unbidden, with more drinks.

When they were all settled, a few seconds of awkward silence ensued.

Then McCallum turned to Grady. "Oh, Fletcher, I've been figuring out a way we might get an additional tax concession on the . . ."

Preston interrupted with a mock groan. "Caleb, please! No work this weekend. It's supposed to be a rest, for all of us. That includes you. Give the boy a break."

Caleb grunted. "Oh, all right." He looked at Grady. "Talk to you about it Monday."

"Okay, sir."

Louise said: "Press, you don't know what you've done."

"What do you mean, Louise?" He sounded a trifle apprehensive.

"If you're not going to let Caleb work at all over the weekend, poor Miss Vickers will have nothing to do. You know Caleb only invited her along to help him in business matters. The child will be bored to tears."

"Oh, don't worry about me, Mrs. McCallum," Ashley

said. "I could never be bored in a heavenly place like this. I'm just so grateful to Mr. Giles for inviting me."

McCallum got abruptly to his feet. "Give it a break, Louise, will you? I'm going indoors to change. 'Scuse me." He strode off.

There was another pause and then Grady rose. "Kitt, how about a walk around the grounds?"

"Yes, love it." She jumped up.

"Oh, do you mind if I come along?" Ashley asked. She, too, got to her feet.

Grady looked a bit disconcerted. But Kitt said quickly: "No, we'd be delighted, wouldn't we, Grady?"

"Oh yes, of course."

"Excuse us," said Kitt.

Grady, Kitt, and Ashley walked off together. As soon as they'd gotten out of sight of the three people they'd left behind, Ashley said: "All right, you two, don't worry. I only wanted an excuse to get away from that . . . that *dear* lady. I'm going to change and have a swim. Cool off. See you."

She hurried away. Grady stared after her.

"I think I'm beginning to like that girl," he said.

Kitt took his arm. "No, you're not. You can't stand her. Come on, I thought you wanted a walk."

Back on the terrace, Preston was saying: "Louise, I want you to know that in spite of what Ashley said, I *didn't* invite her. Well, I suppose I did. What I mean is, Caleb asked if he could bring her. I just said okay."

"That's all right, Press. I realize you couldn't say no."

She turned to Jessica. "Tell me, my dear, who are you coming as tonight? We don't want to duplicate."

Jessica looked puzzled. "Coming as? I'm afraid I don't follow."

"Oh, don't say he hasn't told you! Really, Press, that wasn't very fair on the poor woman."

"I'm sorry!" He threw his hands up in despair. "Believe it or not, I just clean forgot."

"I'm still not in the picture," said Jessica.

"Well, I was talked into making tonight's party a fancy dress affair. Everyone's to come as his favorite fictional character."

Jessica pursed her lips. "Oh, I see."

"I know, and you haven't got a thing to wear."

"Well, actually," Jessica said slowly, "that doesn't really matter."

"Oh?"

They both stared at her.

"You see, my favorite character—female character, that is—has always been Lady Godiva."

Giles and Louise both burst out laughing. Then Jessica snapped her fingers in vexation. "Oh, dear!"

"What's the matter?" Louise asked.

"I've just remembered Lady Godiva's not fictional. So I am in trouble."

Louise put her hand on Jessica's and chuckled. "Anyway, Jessica, wherever would you get all that hair?" She stood up. "Come and see me later. I'm sure between us we can work something out."

She left them and went indoors. Jessica stared after her thoughtfully.

"Penny for them," Preston said.

"I was only thinking how different she seemed just at the end again. Quite pleasant."

"She always used to be like that. She and Caleb both did. One of the nicest couples you could imagine. But then . . ." He shrugged.

"What a shame. Was it when he became rich?"

"I don't think it was *being* that spoiled things. It was the getting of it. I hope before you leave you see Caleb as he once was. Otherwise, you're going to think my friends no better than all those people you fled New York to get away from."

Chapter Four

THE party was in full swing and Preston Giles' house swarmed with characters from what seemed to Jessica every play, book, and film ever written: Hamlet to Rooster Cogburn; Eliza Doolittle to Modesty Blaise. Many people enacted characters from children's stories, nursery rhymes, or comic strips. There was a Superman, a Batman, and a Little Orphan Annie. There were Jacks and Jills and Little Bo-Peeps, Humpty Dumpty, and a Peter Pan (female) escorted by a villainous Captain Hook. A plethora of Disney creations roamed the premises.

Jessica stood near the foot of the stairs, surveying the crowd. She herself was simply but effectively attired in a white evening dress with a tiara, and she carried a silver wand topped with a star.

Intriguing, she thought, the characters people admitted to being their favorites. That young man at the piano, for instance. He was wearing a black and threadbare early Victorian suit and was improvising a song, the refrain of which was based on the words *Bah—humbug*. Ebenezer Scrooge, of course. But could Scrooge be anyone's favorite character? A handsome young man, too, though with a somewhat sardonic expression.

Jessica let her eyes wander on around the room. There was Ashley, looking darkly beautiful as the wicked witch from "Snow White." And there, Caleb McCallum, wearing the familiar cloak and deerstalker hat of Sherlock Holmes and puffing on a meerschaum. He was standing with a group of people and next to a very pretty Little Red Riding Hood. As Jessica watched, McCallum's arm encircled the girl's waist. The girl moved slightly nearer him. Jessica realized that she wasn't the only one who had noticed the incident. Ashley was also watching, and Jessica saw her eyes narrow coldly. Then she turned hastily and made her way across to the piano. Jessica followed unobtrusively.

The sardonic young man was now singing some lines about delighting in sleet and ice. Ashley leaned up against the piano and listened for a moment before interrupting.

"Aren't you a little out of season, Peter? It's not Christmas."

"Wrong, Ashley," he answered curtly. "It's never inappropriate to wish the world a little ill will."

He broke off and looked around the small group who had been listening to him.

"Well, folks, any requests?" With no immediate response forthcoming, he addressed a middle-aged man who was there with his wife. "How about you, Doctor? A medley of my hit from yesteryear, perhaps?"

The doctor spread his hands. "Whatever you like, Peter. Your stuff's all terrific."

Peter smiled icily. "Your taste is impeccable, Doctor. I may get deathly ill, just to cement our relationship."

The doctor said hastily: "What's this I hear about your putting together a new Broadway show?"

"*Off*-Broadway, my friend. The fringes of the civilized world. To be specific—Seventeenth Street."

He smashed his hands down onto the keys in a sudden, jarring discord. Then he seemed to collect himself and started to play normally again.

A voice spoke softly in Jessica's ear. "I'm flabbergasted. Is this what you improvised from odds and ends?"

Jessica turned. It was Preston. She smiled. "With a little help from Louise," she said. "And before you ask—I'm Cinderella's fairy godmother. Would you care to make a wish?"

He took her hand and kissed her fingers. "I wish for a dozen more books by J. B. Fletcher."

"Oh, books aren't produced by magic. Only by hard work."

"Then suppose I just settle for the pleasure of her company."

"That's an easy wish to grant, especially to someone looking as dashing as you. Excuse my ignorance, but who precisely are you?"

He stepped back and struck a pose. "Guess."

Jessica regarded him with her head to one side. "Let me see. Nineteenth century."

"Correct."

"And obviously from the very cream of society. A nobleman."

"Mais oui, madame."

"Ah—French. Someone from Dumas?"

"Bravo."

"Edmond Dantes?"

"Well done. I must admit I'm relieved I look the part. After all, if the host can't manage to get himself in character . . ." He lowered his voice. "Some of them are rather unimaginative, don't you think?"

45

"Yes, and some rather strange. That young man at the piano, now. Who is he, by the way?"

"That's Peter Brill. He's a composer and songwriter."

"So I gathered."

"He had several hits on Broadway a few years back, but he's been going through a lean period, poor fellow. He's scared his talents have gone for good."

"So, he sees himself as a notorious miser, hoarding what he's got and rather hating the world. I see . . ."

"Aren't you being rather Freudian, Jessica? People might come as a particular character for any reason. Maybe just convenience."

"Perhaps you're right."

"And, incidentally, I'm particularly disappointed in Grady and Kitt. They're dressed in perfectly standard evening clothes. Definitely cheating."

"That's what I said. But Grady pointed out that his favorite characters are detectives or secret agents—all of whom dress quite normally."

Preston chuckled. "Where *are* those two, anyway? I haven't seen them around for a long time."

"Nor have I," replied Jessica.

"I expect they've found something better to do."

At that moment Grady and Kitt were in fact locked in a close embrace in the near darkness outside the house. Eventually, however, they drew apart.

"Look," Grady said, "what d'you say we duck out?"

"We can't yet." She took his hand, felt for his watch, and pressed the button that lit up the dial. "It's only nine-fifteen."

"I hate parties," he said.

"Look, *my* boss is giving it; *your* boss is a guest. At least pretend you enjoy their company."

"I like yours better," Grady said with a grin.

"Besides, I'm freezing."

"Oh well, in that case . . ."

He took her in his arms and held her close. As he did so, he happened to glance up at the great mass of the house, and he suddenly stiffened.

"What's the matter?" she asked.

"Look! I think somebody's searching one of the rooms."

She turned and stared. The upper stories were all in darkness. But through one window she could see the faint, jerky movements of a flashlight.

She drew her breath in. "A thief!"

"Got to be. And hang on . . ."

He broke off and appeared to be making some rapid calculations.

Then he gasped. "It's *my* room!"

He suddenly broke away from her and started to sprint to the house.

Kitt ran after him. "Grady—be careful!"

Grady rushed past the open french doors into the noisy living room. He pushed his way roughly through the crowd and started up the stairs two at a time.

Jessica and Preston, still standing talking, stared at him in amazement.

"What on earth . . . ?" Preston began.

"Grady!" Jessica called.

He shouted some reply, which they couldn't catch, but didn't pause.

At that moment Kitt came stumbling into the room. She glanced around, disoriented for a moment, then spotted Preston and Jessica and hurried across to them.

"Grady thinks there's a thief in his room," she panted. "Someone with a flashlight—searching."

47

Without a word, Preston put down his glass, strode to the stairs, and started rapidly up them. Jessica and Kitt followed.

Every eye in the room was on them, and there was a hush until Brill, at the piano, broke into some unmistakable cowboy chase music. Without pausing, he called across the room to McCallum: "Looks like you may be needed, Sherlock."

In the corridor leading to his room Grady stopped. Little point in hurrying now. No one could get out without being seen. He stood still for a few seconds, catching his breath, then tiptoed to his bedroom door and put his ear against it. He could hear nothing. He only hoped he had the right room.

Grady put his hand on the knob, then threw the door open and stepped into the room.

He'd made no mistake. A shadowy figure near the window swung around as he entered.

"Don't move!" Grady groped for the light switch.

But he wasn't familiar with its exact position, and as he fumbled, he was suddenly blinded by the flashlight shining directly into his eyes.

The intruder was coming straight at him, as if intending to brush him aside by sheer brute force.

Grady braced himself, raised his fists, and then at the last moment stepped aside and ducked. Instantly he was out of the beam of light, and behind the hand that held the flashlight he was able to discern the dim outline of the intruder.

Grady straightened and delivered a powerful left jab at the man's midriff. It brought him up short with a gasp and Grady aimed a right at his jaw.

The man jerked his head back, and this time Grady's fist

caught him only a glancing blow. However, it was enough to send him staggering backward through the open doorway into the corridor—where he cannoned violently into Preston, who was just arriving.

Both men went sprawling, with Preston underneath. The unknown man, though, was quickly on his feet and, before Grady could reach the doorway, was off like a jackrabbit.

Grady charged to the door and saw the man's back disappearing along the corridor. Ahead of him, frozen in the center of the passage, were Jessica and Kitt.

Grady gave a yell. "Get out of his way!"

In a flash Jessica jumped to one side, grabbing Kitt by the arm as she did so. They flattened themselves against the wall.

As the man approached them he raised his arm as if to cover his face. Then he was level with them, still sprinting at full speed.

The next second there was a sudden flash of silver across the corridor, and the man went sprawling. He lay dazed as Jessica calmly bent down and picked up her wand, now broken in the middle, with which she'd deftly tripped him.

Grady came running up. "Well done, Aunt Jess!"

He bent down, grabbed the man by the back of his jacket, and hauled him unceremoniously to his feet.

At that moment Preston, obviously none the worse for his tumble, came hurrying up. At the same time there could be heard, from the direction of the stairs, a rising buzz of conversation, as of the sound of approaching locusts, together with the muffled tramp of many feet on deep-pile carpet. It was clear that all the other guests had decided to investigate the mysterious and noisy happenings aloft.

Preston shot a glance at Kitt. "Kitt, tell them everything's under control, nothing to worry about. Take 'em back downstairs and make sure they stay there. Get 'em playing blindman's buff, if necessary.''

"Right, Mr. Giles.''

Kitt turned to Jessica and gave a little grimace. She muttered, "Who'd be in PR work?'' and hurried off.

Preston directed his attention to the intruder, still tightly held in Grady's grip. Having apparently recovered his breath, the man spoke for the first time. And he spoke with surprising dignity.

"All right, young man, that's enough. You can release me. There's no need to be boorish.''

Preston and Jessica stared at him in surprise. Grady grinned.

"Nothing doing, pal. Not until I know what you were up to in my room.''

"Jessica,'' Preston said, "would you be so kind as to call the police? The nearest phone is in my bedroom. Fourth door on the right.''

"Certainly.''

Jessica moved off, only to stop as the man barked sharply. "Wait!''

He addressed Preston. "Before you take so irremediable a step, you would be well advised to listen to what I have to say.''

Preston hesitated, then, to Jessica's surprise, glanced at her and raised his eyebrows, as if asking her advice.

She said slowly: "I suppose it would do no harm.''

The man gave her a little bow. "Thank you, madam.''

"Very well,'' Preston said. "We'll *all* go to my bedroom. Can you manage him, Grady?''

"I think so, sir.'' He gave the intruder a shove. "Move.''

"Really, this manhandling is totally unnecessary,'' the newcomer said stiffly.

"We'll decide that," Preston told him.

They reached Preston's bedroom. He opened the door, switched on the light, and then stood back to allow Grady to march the intruder in. Jessica followed. Finally, Preston himself went in. He closed the door, turned the key in the lock, pocketed it, then walked across to the intruder and rapidly frisked him.

"I am not armed," the man said coldly.

"So I see." Preston stepped back. "Grady, I think you can release the . . . er, gentleman now."

"Thank you at least for the courtesy of that word," the man said, as Grady released him and stepped away.

In the brighter light of Preston's bedroom they were able for the first time to get a good look at the intruder. He was of middle age and, in spite of his somewhat disheveled appearance, had an indefinably elegant air about him. He was wearing a three-piece suit, which he was in the act of brushing down with his hands, and a slightly askew silk tie. He certainly did not fit Jessica's mental image of an average burglar.

"Well," Preston snapped after a few seconds, "we're waiting."

"A moment."

The man took from his pocket a silk handkerchief and with it gently dabbed at a cut on his lip. He regarded the small spot of blood left on the handkerchief, sighed, and returned it to his pocket.

"My name," he responded at last, "is Dexter Baxendale. I am a private detective."

"A *what?*" Preston exclaimed.

"I believe I made myself quite clear."

"You're kidding," Grady said incredulously.

Baxendale turned a supercilious gaze on him. "Not

everyone in my profession sports a broken nose and dirty fingernails, my pubescent friend. When society seeks confidential assistance, it does not necessarily hire Mike Hammer.''

He reached into his vest pocket, produced a business card, and handed it to Preston.

Preston gave it a cursory glance. ''This does not explain what you are doing here.''

''I have been retained by a very influential individual to conduct a discreet investigation. With Dexter Baxendale, discretion is a way of life.''

''You still haven't answered my question,'' Preston said. ''What are you doing *here?*''

''I'm not at liberty to say.''

Preston gave a sigh. He crossed to the telephone, lifted the receiver, and started to dial.

Baxendale said sharply: ''You may turn me over to the local authorities, Mr. Giles, but no amount of coercion will force me to break a trust. On the other hand, when the newspapers latch onto this story, a finger of suspicion will point equally at each of your guests. Which one is under investigation? Need I warn you, the *Enquirer* will have a field day?''

Preston hesitated, then lowered the receiver. He stood in thought for a moment before reaching a decision. ''Grady,'' he said, ''will you do me a favor? Escort Mr. Baxendale to his car.''

''Sure thing, Mr. Giles.''

''And out the *back* way, please. I'd rather not disturb our guests any further.'' He went to the door, unlocked and opened it.

Baxendale turned to Jessica and again gave his little bow. ''A pleasure meeting you, Mrs. Fletcher, even though our conversation has been somewhat limited. You have a rare gift for murder. Continued success.''

"Thank you," Jessica said. Then she added: "I think."

Grady tapped Baxendale's arm. "Let's go."

Baxendale started for the door, then stopped. His eye fell upon a small statuette, about a foot high, standing on a shelf. He went toward it and inspected it more closely. In brass, it represented Blind Justice, her scale unevenly balanced. A smile suddenly crossed Baxendale's lips and he looked again at Preston.

"Forgive me, Mr. Giles," he said, "but since I first entered this room, I've been trying to deduce who you're dressed as, and I think I have it. Edmond Dantes, isn't it? Otherwise known as the Count of Monte Cristo?"

Preston raised his eyebrows. "Very good, Mr. Baxendale. I'm almost sorry I'm throwing you out. You might have made a charming guest."

Baxendale smiled again, then he and Grady went out. As Grady turned to close the door behind him, Preston called out, "Grady, thanks a lot. Very well done."

Grady grinned. "Any time, Mr. Giles, any time." He closed the door.

Preston turned to Jessica. "I think, in fact, that all this has made your nephew's day."

"I wouldn't be at all surprised."

"What did I promise you? A quiet weekend?"

"I get plenty of quiet back in Cabot Cove. I won't say the incident has made *my* day, but it's certainly presented something to think about."

"Jessica, don't tell me that fiendishly clever brain of yours is beginning to feel the stirrings of a new plot?"

"Too soon to say. But isn't that what you want?"

"Yes, but I'm not sure *I* want to be a character in your next book."

"Do you realize," Grady said, "that guy was a private detective?"

"So you just told me," said Kitt. She and Grady were in the living room, standing slightly apart from the other party guests.

"A P.I. A gumshoe. Like Philip Marlowe, Sam Spade, Dick Tracy."

"So?"

"So, *I* flattened him. And I'm just an accountant."

"I know, darling, terrific."

"Yes, but don't you see: it opens up the possibility of a whole new fiction genre. There have never been any thrillers with an accountant as hero. Imagine a TV series: *The Fighting CPA*. Or how about *The Fastest Auditor in the West?* Every week there's an uppity young punk accountant who tries to take his title away. Imagine the drama as they battle against each other and the clock. Sensation: our hero loses. But wait—the punk's figures don't balance. One cent is unaccounted for. The good triumphs. Or . . ."

"Grady."

"Yes, Kitt?"

"Shut up."

"Yes, Kitt."

"You were great. I'm very proud of you. But the fact is, you still don't know why that man was in *your* room."

"Probably doing the rounds of all the bedrooms. I just happened to spot him when he'd reached mine."

"Could be, I suppose."

But Kitt sounded doubtful.

"Oh, there's Mr. Giles and Aunt Jess," Grady observed.

"I'd better go and report that Baxendale's gone. 'Scuse me a moment."

He crossed the room and engaged Preston in conversation. While they were talking, Jessica heard her name called. She turned and saw Caleb McCallum beckoning her. He was standing with Ashley, the doctor, and one or two other people she didn't know. She went across.

"Mrs. Fletcher," McCallum said loudly, "the doc here's been saying there's things I could do to make my Chowder Houses better. But if there's one thing I know, it's the public taste bud. They want their food fast and cheap. Now, you're from Maine. You know fish. You ever eaten at a Cap'n Caleb's?"

"I have indeed, Captain," said Jessica. "And I must say it was an experience I shall never forget."

McCallum looked pleased. "I rest my case."

The doctor gave Jessica the ghost of a wink and Jessica smiled back. Would this be a good chance to support the doctor and give Cap'n Caleb *her* suggestions for improvements?

She opened her mouth to disabuse him as to her meaning. But she never got the words out, for suddenly McCallum's expression of satisfaction was replaced by one of extreme irritation. However, his look was not directed at Jessica, but over her shoulder.

Jessica looked behind her. Approaching them with a very unsteady gait was Louise.

She reached the group, leaned on a table for support, and stared at her husband.

"The party's beginning to pall, Caleb," she said loudly, her words slightly slurred. "Let's go home."

McCallum regarded his wife coldly. "Get yourself some coffee, Louise."

"I don't want coffee. I want to go home."

"I don't," he said fiercely.

The other guests in the immediate vicinity had all been looking slightly embarrassed and edging away. Now only Jessica was nearby.

Louise smiled sweetly at Caleb. "Fine, darling, you stay. I'll trot off like a civilized wife and let you and Ashley do whatever it is you do."

She turned and lurched away. Jessica hesitated for a few moments, glanced at McCallum, who had dismissively turned his back, then went after Louise herself.

Just inside the front door, Louise stopped and began fumbling in her purse. As Jessica came up to her, she produced her car key.

Jessica put a hand on her arm. "Louise, please don't go," she said gently. "Not just yet."

Louise pulled away, zigzagged to the door, opened it, and went out into the darkness.

Jessica sighed. "Oh, dear."

She looked around helplessly. Then her eye alighted on Grady, who was making his way back to Kitt. Jessica hurried across to him.

"Grady, be a good boy and help Mrs. McCallum home."

He looked a little disgruntled and glanced toward Kitt. "But . . ."

"I know we're all using you tonight," Jessica said hastily, "but this is important. In her condition, Louise really shouldn't drive. She won't take any notice of me—and you're one of the few completely sober people here."

He nodded. "I see. Sure." He turned and hurried out.

In the open air he paused, peering around. There seemed to be dozens of cars parked on the circular driveway, and the only light came from the windows of the house behind him.

Then he spotted Louise's figure weaving through the cars, and he started forward.

By the time he caught up with her, she had reached a Cadillac sedan. She placed her hand on the catch of the driver's door.

"Hi, Mrs. McCallum," he called cheerfully.

She peered suspiciously at him. "Who's that?"

"Me. Grady Fletcher." He went closer. "How about letting me drive you home?"

She shook her head dazedly. "Do I know you?"

"Sure you do. I work for the firm. The promising young man, remember?"

"Promising? Well, promise me something now, eh?"

"What's that?"

"To clear off and leave me alone."

"But it'll be no trouble. Just let me have the key."

He leaned forward, but she suddenly screamed at him hysterically. "I said, leave me alone!"

At the same time, she swung open the car door so violently that he had to step clear hastily. While he was still off-balance, she shoved him in the chest with both hands. He staggered backward and sat down hard on the gravel.

Before he could recover, she jumped into the Cadillac and started the engine. As he scrambled to his feet, the car shot away in a cascade of spraying gravel and spinning tires.

Grady stared after it and swore under his breath.

"Grady, are you all right?"

Jessica trotted solicitously up to him. Kitt was a few steps behind her.

"Yes, fine," he said. "It's her I'm worried about. She's crazy. Did you hear how she yelled at me?"

"I did. I'm sorry to have let you in for all that. Perhaps I shouldn't have interfered. However, I *am* going to tell her husband what's happened. After that, there's nothing more I can do." She started back toward the house.

Kitt edged up to Grady and took him by the arm. "Sure you're all right?"

"Yes, of course."

They started off after Jessica. "I've been thinking," Kitt said. "This TV series—*The Fighting CPA*—will there be an episode in which *he's* flattened by a middle-aged female drunk?"

"Aw, I hate a smart-aleck broad," said Grady.

Chapter Five

ON entering the house, Jessica located Caleb McCallum in a side room, where he was exerting all his not overabundant charm on Little Red Riding Hood. Jessica told him of Louise's departure. He thanked her perfunctorily, but clearly couldn't care less.

Jessica sighed and returned to the party. It was still going with a swing. More and more people seemed to be learning of her identity, and she found herself quite a center of attraction. This was not greatly to her taste, and—after having been asked for the eighth time in a little over half an hour, "How on earth did you think up the plot?"—was soon seeking a means of escape from the limelight. It was just after ten-thirty and the revelry was plainly going on for hours yet.

Then she noticed that Peter Brill had again been persuaded, not with great difficulty, to return to the piano. More from a desire to fade into the background than from any intense wish to hear him perform, Jessica joined the small crowd that had gathered around him.

"Thirty dollars a ticket?" the man dressed as Humpty Dumpty was declaiming. "I'm sorry, Peter, at those prices, off Broadway is beyond my budget."

"And you know what it takes to mount a new produc-

59

tion?'' Brill said bitterly. ''A quarter million barely gets you started. Ah well, if this new show fails, I can always write for Nashville.''

Half on key, he started to sing in an exaggerated country and western style:

> She was Queen of office sweethearts,
> He was the King that brought her to ruin,
> He gave her dictation and a place to stay,
> Then he gave her a royal . . .

At that point he noticed Ashley, who had come from the bar.

''Oops,'' he said, ''sorry, Ashley, no offense intended.''

''None taken,'' she said coolly. ''For the past several months my relationship with the Captain has been strictly business.''

Jessica eyed her thoughtfully. Brill shrugged and played two other tunes. Then he took another drink and surveyed the room. ''By the way, where *is* Sherlock? I haven't seen him for quite a while.''

''You haven't seen Little Red Riding Hood either, I'll be bound,'' said Ashley. ''Maybe she's taken him to investigate the murder at Grandmother's house.'' She raised her glass. ''Here's to crime.''

Just as she was about to drink, someone passing behind jostled her, and most of the contents of the glass cascaded down the front of her dress.

She gave an exclamation of annoyance.

Jessica bustled forward. ''Quickly, my dear, we'd better get that out before it stains.''

''Oh, forget it,'' said Ashley.

"Nonsense, that's much too good a dress to ruin. Come with me."

She took Ashley firmly by the wrist and led her in the direction of the kitchen.

In the kitchen they found Preston. He was on the phone. As they entered, he was saying: ". . . please, I don't want Mrs. Fletcher bothered."

He turned, saw Jessica and Ashley, and made a wry grimace before saying into the phone: "All right, then, I'll see you." He listened for a few seconds, then added: "Very well," and hung up.

As he came away from the phone, he noticed the state of Ashley's dress. "An accident?"

"Nothing serious," Jessica told him. "Was that about me?"

"Yes—a very persistent reporter from the *New York Times*. Name of Chris Landon. He wants to interview you on Monday."

"What did you tell him?"

"Well, knowing how you felt about the press, I explained that you'd left for Pago Pago and weren't expected back until the turn of the century. Unfortunately, he didn't believe me. I've arranged to see him, but I don't think that'll satisfy him."

"The *New York Times*, after all," said Jessica, *"is* in a somewhat different league from some of the others."

While speaking, she had gone across to the cabinets and started rummaging through them. "Hope you don't mind," she said, retrieving a large mixing bowl and a box of baking soda.

"Be my guest."

He and Ashley watched fascinated as she went to the fridge, gradually unearthing two eggs and a quart of milk.

"I don't know what that's going to be," said Preston, "but I'm not eating any."

"It's an old Fletcher recipe," she explained, piling the ingredients into the bowl. "Guaranteed to take the spots off a leopard. Come on, Ashley, we'll go upstairs."

"Jessica, really," Ashley insisted, "it isn't worth the trouble."

"I'm a frugal Yankee. Humor me."

She led Ashley out of the kitchen. Really, Jessica thought, what with one thing and another, this is an extremely busy evening. But interesting. Yes, undeniably so . . .

Although she was very late getting to sleep that night, Jessica nevertheless woke early. Feeling surprisingly fresh, she got up and pulled back the curtains. It was another glorious day.

Much too glorious, in fact, to go back to bed. How fortunate that she'd brought her jogging outfit with her.

Ten minutes later Jessica went downstairs. She could hear one of the servants clearing up the horrible detritus left by the party, but everybody else was clearly still in bed.

Resisting the impulse to go in and offer to help with the clearing up (whatever would Davis think?), Jessica let herself out and started off down the drive. She jogged about a mile, enjoying the freshness of the air in her lungs and on her cheeks, and then turned and made her way back toward the house.

When she was halfway up the drive again, she heard behind her the sound of a car. She looked over her shoulder and saw that it was the McCallum Cadillac. Louise was at the wheel. She pulled up alongside Jessica and let down the window. She was wearing the same clothes as the previous night. She looked terrible—with hair awry, makeup smeared, eyes bleary, and complexion gray.

"Good morning, Louise," Jessica said. "You . . ."

Louise raised a hand. "Don't say it. However dismal I look, I assure you I feel a hundred times worse. Get in, Jessica, will you?"

Jessica opened the door and scrambled in beside her. Louise surveyed her without enthusiasm. Jessica smiled. "We were very worried about you last night."

"*We?*"

"Grady and Kitt and I. And Preston when I told him later."

"Tell me, Jessica: did I behave very badly?"

"I wouldn't say so. A lot of people had too much to drink and became a little obstreperous."

Louise gave a harsh laugh. "That's a nice way to put it. What about your nephew? Did I knock him down, or something?"

"There was a slight accident with the car door, that's all. He just stumbled. No harm done."

Louise rested her head on her hands, which were crossed on the wheel. "No, that's not true. I pushed him over. I remember. I screamed at him. And I made a fool of myself indoors, about Caleb and that girl."

"Look, let's go up to the house and have some coffee."

Louise shook her head. "Oh no, I don't want to hang around any longer than I have to. I just wanted to see Caleb, and I thought perhaps at this hour everyone else would still be in bed. Caleb did sleep here last night, didn't he?"

"Well, I don't know," Jessica said a little awkwardly. "After you left I rather lost track of him."

"He went off somewhere?"

"Not necessarily. And if he did, he may have come back

after I went to bed. Perhaps he borrowed a car and went looking for you.''

"Don't try and kid me, Jessica. I was the last person he wanted to see.''

"Maybe he's gone home. Have you been there?''

"No. At least, I'm pretty sure I haven't. The last thing I remember is driving away from here. This morning I woke just before sunup behind the wheel of the car. On the beach.''

"Let's see if he is at the house now. If not, you can phone home. Or I will for you, if you like.''

Louise rubbed her eyes. "Very well. And thanks, Jessica. It's a waste of time, though. He's with some floozie. I don't know why I expected to find him here. Still a bit fuddled, I guess.''

They drove up the rest of the driveway and got out of the car. Before they reached the front door, utterly without warning, from somewhere came a nerve-shattering, piercing scream.

The two women froze. "Who the . . .'' Louise asked shakily.

Jessica thought a second. "That seemed to come from the pool.'' She turned and ran in the direction of the sound. Louise stared after her.

Approaching the pool area, Jessica rounded a corner of the house, where she ran full tilt into Kitt. The girl was wearing a swimsuit—and sobbing hysterically.

"Kitt, my dear! What on earth's the matter?'' Jessica took her by the shoulders.

"The pool,'' Kitt gasped, "the pool.''

"What about it?''

"He's . . . he's . . . Oh no! It's horrible!''

She shook Jessica off, covered her face with her hands, and leaned up against the wall, sobbing.

Jessica eyed her for a second, then took a deep breath. She walked resolutely up to the edge of the pool and looked in.

Floating on the surface of the water was a man. And his face . . .

Jessica turned her head aside with a shudder. Where his face had been there was now . . . nothing. Nothing but . . .

Jessica somehow managed to fight down her nausea and forced herself to take another look.

Spread out like a water mattress under the man's body was a grimly familiar Victorian cloak. And on his head— what was left of his head—was a deerstalker hat.

Again Jessica averted her eyes. She had seen all she needed.

She became aware of a patch of red near her feet and looked down. It was blood. She stepped hastily away from it. And her foot came in contact with an object she had half noticed before, but which had barely registered on her mind. It was the skeet gun.

At that moment she heard running footsteps behind her. She spun to see Louise approaching. Jessica stepped toward her, throwing up her arms.

"No, Louise!"

But it was no use. Louise ignored her and half stumbled up to the edge of the pool. She looked in and gave a choking gasp of revulsion.

Then she screamed just one word:

"Caleb!"

Chapter Six

POLICE Chief Roy Gunderson was a cigar-smoking, gray-haired man in his early fifties. The main impression he made on Preston Giles was of a man intensely irritated at having been called to investigate an early Sunday morning crime. The police chief, Preston felt, resented his thoughtlessness in hosting a party on Saturday rather than Sunday. Otherwise, when guests began knocking one another off, the chief could have commenced his murder investigation in the proper and tidy way, on Monday morning.

"It *is* murder, then—quite definitely?" Preston asked him, trying to ignore the impression.

They were in Preston's study. The photographers and fingerprint experts had done their work. The body had been briefly examined and taken away. The routine of criminal investigation was well under way. And it was still not nine a.m.

Gunderson took a much-chewed cigar from his mouth. "Nobody, but nobody, blows his own face to pulp with a twelve-gauge shotgun, Mr. Giles."

Preston winced. "Perhaps not, but an accident . . . ?"

"Difficult to make those guns go off by accident. You can drop 'em, throw 'em down even. Besides."

As Preston waited, Gunderson deliberately relit his cigar, then brought out his *pièce de résistance*. "There's no prints on the gun. It's been wiped clean."

Preston said: "Oh."

"Now, maybe Captain McCallum and somebody else were foolin' around and the other person picked up the gun and pulled the trigger, not knowing it was loaded. And then panicked. Or maybe McCallum attacked someone who shot him in self-defense. That could make it manslaughter or justifiable homicide. That's for the courts to decide. Somebody did it, and they're concealing the fact. In my book, that makes it a murder inquiry. No matter the reason it happened."

Preston shrugged. "As you say, Chief."

Gunderson took out his notebook. "Now, I want to get clear who's who in this place. Seems the first three people to see the body—within a couple of minutes of each other— were all da . . . er, ladies. Right?"

"I believe so."

"A Miss Kitt Donovan, a Mrs. Jessica Fletcher, and the dead man's wife—widow—Louise. That was shortly after six a.m. Kind of early to be up on a Sunday morning, wasn't it? Especially after a late-night party?"

"You'll have to ask them about that."

"Oh, I will, Mr. Giles. I've seen your doctor friend, who first examined the body, and he says I can't speak to Miss Donovan or the widow yet. They had bad shocks and he insisted they go and lie down. But it seems this Mrs. Fletcher's made of sterner stuff."

"Well, she is J. B. Fletcher, you know—the author of *The Corpse Danced at Midnight*. My firm published it."

An expression of disgust came over Gunderson's face. "Aw, mystery writers! They make me sick! Thinking up these impossible, crazy crimes, and making the police out a lot of dopes.''

He stubbed out his cigar viciously. ''Where is she, anyway? I want to see her.''

''She was in the living room with my other guests. Shall we go in?''

In the living room they found Grady, Peter Brill, Ashley Vickers, and the doctor. There was no sign of Jessica, but Davis was serving coffee.

Preston looked around. ''Where's your aunt gone, Grady?''

''I think she's outside.''

''Thanks. Want to come and find her, Chief?''

But Gunderson's eyes were on the steaming liquid being dispensed by Davis. Preston spotted this.

''Coffee, Chief?''

Gunderson glanced at his watch. ''Yeah, thanks. I could use some. Guess Mrs. Fletcher will keep.''

Davis handed him a cup and he sipped with relish, while Preston performed introductions.

''Doc,'' Gunderson said, ''I know you're not the coroner, but you did look at the body. How long d'you figure he'd been dead?''

The doctor pursed his lips. ''Hard to say accurately without a proper examination. But several hours, at least.''

''In other words, he was probably killed while your party was going on, Mr. Giles. Yet nobody heard a shot. From a twelve-gauge shotgun?''

Preston said: ''You have to remember, Chief, the party was noisy. It gets chilly at night, so the windows were closed. And the pool *is* some distance from the house.''

Gunderson grunted. ''What's the last time any of you saw him?''

They looked at each other. At last Ashley broke the silence. "I was talking to him and several other people about ten before ten. Then Louise came up and said she wanted to go home. You were there, Doctor."

The doctor nodded.

Ashley went on: "Louise was somewhat the worse for drink. Caleb—Captain McCallum—told her to go and get some coffee. She stormed off on her own. A minute or so later the Captain drifted away. I didn't see him after that."

"Did anybody else?" Gunderson studied their faces. There was a general shaking of heads. "What happened to Mrs. McCallum?"

Grady supplied the answer. "She drove off almost at once."

"Somewhat the worse for drink?"

Grady shrugged. "We tried to stop her, but it was no use."

"And," Preston said, "she didn't get back here until a few minutes before the body was found."

Gunderson rounded on him. "You know that for a fact, Mr. Giles?"

"Well, not exactly, but Mrs. Fletcher told me, just before you arrived . . ."

Gunderson interrupted. "Never mind what Mrs. Fletcher told you. I'll be talking to her. And to all the guests, I suppose." He cast his eyes upward. "Gee, what a job! Nine out of ten of 'em will have been half-soused . . ."

He wandered over to the window and put his cup on the ledge. "Okay, we'll leave opportunity for the moment. What about motive? Somebody got any preliminary ideas about that?"

Peter Brill spoke for the first time. "A motive for killing

Caleb McCallum? Surely you jest, sir. Half the country had reason to kill the man, and the other half didn't know him.''

Gunderson scowled at him. "Not funny, friend.''

"But accurate,'' Ashley said calmly. "The Captain was not particularly well loved, though I doubt if any of us despised him enough to kill him.''

"Except for me, of course.''

The voice came from the door. They all jerked around to face Louise. She was deathly pale.

The doctor got to his feet and hurried toward her. "Mrs. McCallum, you ought to be resting. You should have let me give you a sedative.''

She waved him away. "I'm all right, Doctor, thank you.''

She came fully into the room. "Did I shock you? But it's what you're all thinking, isn't it?''

"Louise,'' Preston said gently, "I was just telling Chief Gunderson that you left here alone last night and didn't get back until six this morning.''

"That right, Mrs. McCallum?'' Gunderson asked.

"Frankly, I don't know.''

"You don't?''

"No. I'm being quite candid, you see. I don't think I came back, but I don't really remember anything between leaving here and waking up in my car on the beach this morning. But I did not kill my husband, Mr. Gunderson.''

"But if you don't remember anything that happened between . . .''

"Well, I do think, don't you, that however drunk I was, I would remember a thing like that?''

Gunderson stared intently at her for a moment without speaking before turning to pick up his coffee cup. As he did so, he happened to glance out of the window.

A woman was walking along, staring intently up toward

the top of the house, shading her eyes with her hand. Gunderson beckoned to Preston, who joined him at the window.

"Would that be Mrs. Fletcher, by any chance?"

"Yes, that's Jessica."

As they were speaking, Jessica moved to a small flower bed. She got down on her hands and knees, peered closely at the bed, and then gently poked at the soil with her finger.

"What's she up to?" Preston muttered.

Gunderson gave a muted exclamation. "Starting her own private investigation, is my guess. That's all I need! Amateurs!"

He faced the occupants of the room again. "We'll be taking statements from all of you. So keep yourselves available." He made for the door.

Brill said hurriedly, "Chief, I'm holding auditions for a new show. I must be back in town by this evening."

Gunderson stopped and looked at him hard. "You will leave when I say so, Mr. Brill. Not before."

He went out.

Against the wall of the house near the flower bed was some latticework. After rising to her feet, Jessica surveyed it. Then she moved forward, took hold of it, shook it, and started to climb. It supported her weight quite well.

However, she had only gone a couple of feet off the ground, when behind her she heard the sound of throat-clearing. She looked over her shoulder. A gray-haired man was standing a few feet away, staring at her calmly.

"Morning," he said.

"Oh, good morning." Hastily, Jessica climbed down. She felt rather foolish.

"Mrs. Fletcher?"

"That's right."

"Roy Gunderson. Police chief."

"Oh, how do you do, Chief Gunderson." Jessica held out her hand. "Look, I do beg your pardon, but I was just checking something out. I probably should have asked you first. I didn't disturb any evidence, believe me."

Gunderson deliberately took a cigar from his pocket and lit it. "I read your book," he said.

"Oh, did you really? How nice."

"Said I read it. Didn't say I liked it."

"Oh."

"I been talking to some of the others inside. None of them saw McCallum last night after the spat with his wife. Did you?"

"Just immediately after. I told him that she'd left. That was shortly before ten, I think. He wasn't very concerned. After that he disappeared."

"So, what do you think?"

"I beg your pardon?"

"You know people, ma'am. You spot the little things, the inconsistencies. So, what do you think about Mrs. McCallum?"

"Surely she's not a suspect?"

"At the moment she's *the* suspect."

"My goodness."

Jessica started to walk slowly and thoughtfully across the grass, away from the house. Gunderson fell in beside her. She stopped and looked at him. "Chief, did Mr. Giles tell you about the intruder we had here last night?"

"That New York private eye? You think *he* killed the Captain?"

"No, not at all. But I'm sure you noticed the shoes on the body floating in the pool."

"Shoes?"

"They were brown—casual—with soft rubber soles. At the party, the Captain was wearing black patent leather—highly polished."

"That so?"

"The private detective was wearing brown shoes. I noticed them when I tripped him in the corridor. Now, I'm pretty sure he got in through that window."

She pointed upward to a partially opened second-story window. He followed her gaze, then looked down again, as she moved back a few steps to the flower bed.

"Now, look: you see these broken flowers—and over there, that footprint? In order to make the climb to that window, the detective would have had to wear soft, rubber-soled shoes."

Gunderson stared at her. "Mrs. Fletcher, just what are you telling me?"

"Oh, I wouldn't presume to tell you anything, Mr. Gunderson. But, as the face of the man in the pool was not identifiable, it did occur to me that perhaps we were all a little hasty in assuming . . ." She trailed off.

Gunderson's eyes bulged. "You mean . . . the guy in the pool wasn't McCallum?"

"No, he damn well wasn't!"

The voice was stentorian, and they both swung toward it.

Standing alongside the house, accompanied by a young deputy, was Captain Caleb McCallum.

"Well," Roy Gunderson gasped, "I'll be a son of a . . ."

McCallum strode forward, interrupting him rudely. "You *are*, Chief. You always have been. And you're a stupid one, to boot."

Gunderson glowered at him. It was clear that at this moment he was sorry the body was *not* that of Caleb McCallum.

"Is that so?" he snapped. "All right, McCallum, suppose you show how bright you are and tell me who that corpse is, and how come he was wearing your costume."

"I haven't the faintest idea," McCallum said calmly.

"You know all about it, though?"

"Your deputy's just told me."

Before Gunderson could speak again there was an interruption.

"Caleb!"

The voice held a mixture of disbelief and joy. Louise was standing quite still, staring at her husband, her face stained with tears. The next moment she was running toward him. She threw herself against him and flung her arms around his neck.

"Oh, Caleb! Thank God!"

McCallum, looking somewhat embarrassed, gave her a perfunctory embrace.

"It's all right, Louise," he muttered. "I'm fine, just fine."

She drew back and stared up into his face. Then she glanced sideways at Jessica and Gunderson. Her expression was changing. Already, it was possible to believe, she was feeling slightly ashamed of her display of emotion. She looked at her husband again.

"You're really all right?"

"I've said so, haven't I?"

He looked and sounded irritated. And this fact suddenly sank in on Louise. She flushed.

"Is that so?" she said harshly. "Well, I've news for you, Caleb: *I'm not!*"

Without warning, she drew back her arm and dealt him a stinging blow across the cheek.

McCallum stumbled back. "What's that for?" he roared.

"That's for last night. And all the other last nights you've put me through."

Louise turned on her heel and strode away.

Gunderson emitted a muffled snort, heard only by Jessica, and which she was quite sure was suppressed laughter. However, his demeanor was grave as he stepped forward.

"Let's go indoors," he said. "It's time you and I had a serious talk, McCallum."

McCallum hesitated, then gave a curt nod. They started toward the house. Jessica, her face pensive, fell in behind.

Gunderson kept the Captain waiting for a minute or so while he conferred earnestly with the young deputy. Then he accompanied McCallum into the house.

The news of Caleb's resurrection had preceded him—doubtless by way of Louise—and a crowd was waiting to greet him. Of Louise herself there was now no sign.

Preston stepped forward with outstretched hand and beaming face. "Caleb, my dear fellow, this is wonderful! I can hardly believe it."

McCallum took his hand a shade unwillingly. "Thanks, Press."

Ashley approached him. "Good to have you back among the living, Captain McCallum."

"Well, Ashley, actually I'd never left, as you can see."

Brill came toward him and laid a hand affectionately on his shoulder. "Caleb," he said in a voice charged with emotion, "I can't tell you how much this means to me—to be able to see you again, touch you, to know that you're going

75

to be around.'' He gulped. ''I can hardly keep back my tears. Tears of joy, of course.''

McCallum glared at him suspiciously, but Brill's face was perfectly straight.

Gunderson said: ''Mr. Giles, do you mind if I use your study for a bit?''

''No, go right ahead,'' Preston said.

''Thanks. Come along, Mr. McCallum.''

In the study, Gunderson seated himself behind Preston's desk and had McCallum sit facing him. He relit his cigar, gazing at McCallum as he did so. ''What do you know about a guy called Dexter Baxendale?''

McCallum gave a start. ''Baxendale? Well, he's a private detective.''

''And what's he to you?''

''He's been working for me.''

''Doing what?''

''If you must know, I've been having some business problems lately. Somebody in my organization has been leaking confidential information. I hired Baxendale to find out who.''

''And has he?''

''Not yet—as far as I know. Last Friday he told me he was on to something and might have it wrapped up over the weekend. But I haven't heard anything yet. No doubt later today . . .''

''So, what was he doing here last night?''

McCallum looked startled. ''Baxendale was here?''

''You didn't know?''

''No, of course not. Why didn't he report to me? Who did he see?''

''Baxendale was caught by Preston Giles and Grady

Fletcher searching Fletcher's room during the party. Seems he got in through a window.''

McCallum was looking staggered. "I can hardly believe it! I heard there'd been an intruder, but I'd no idea it was Baxendale." He frowned suddenly. "But, look, why are you bringing this up now? I thought you were interested in this body in the pool . . ." He broke off. "Good Lord, you don't mean . . .''

"Mrs. Fletcher seems to think so.''

"Mrs. Fletcher? What on earth's it got to do with her?''

"Smart lady, Mrs. Fletcher," Gunderson said ruminatively. "She spotted the corpse's shoes were a lot like Baxendale's—and not like yours. Anyway, my men are checking the body's fingerprints now, comparing them with the intruder's, lifted from Grady Fletcher's room. We should have a positive ID soon. And while we're waiting, I want answers to a few more questions.''

"Such as?''

"What the dead man was doing in your costume, for one.''

"I've told you I know nothing about that.''

"What happened to the costume? When did you take it off?''

"I don't know exactly. I'd decided to go out for some fresh air.''

Gunderson looked at him skeptically. "Oh, yeah?''

McCallum's jaw was working angrily. "All right, if you must know, I left with a young woman—a guest at the party.''

"Left for where?''

"We, er, spent the night at a local inn. I knew nothing about anything that had happened until I arrived back here and ran into your deputy.''

"That still doesn't explain the Sherlock Holmes costume."

"I took it off and dumped it in the front closet before I left here. I wasn't going to prance into the lobby of that inn looking like a refugee from a costume ball."

"I see." Gunderson nodded slowly. "Well, that makes sense. About the only thing that has so far. What was the name of this girl?"

"Look, Gunderson, do we have to drag her into it?"

"Don't see we have much choice, considering she's your only alibi."

"But you can't suspect me of killing this man. Even if he *is* Baxendale."

"You told me yourself Baxendale had been investigating your company. Suppose he happened to find out something he wasn't meant to, and decided to try a spot of blackmail."

"That's nonsense!"

"Or maybe dug out something about your private life. That's not exactly pure as the driven snow. Oh, that reminds me—the girl's name."

Unwillingly, McCallum muttered, "Tracy something. I don't know her other name. At the party she was dressed as Little Red Riding Hood."

Gunderson made a note. "Thanks. I'll get her full name from Giles."

At that moment there was a tap on the door.

"Yeah?" Gunderson yelled.

The door opened and the young deputy put his head in.

"Yes, Jim?"

"Positive, Chief."

"Thanks, Jim. Quick work."

The deputy went out. McCallum looked at the police chief. "I suppose that means . . ."

Gunderson nodded. "Yup. The guy in the pool *was* Dexter Baxendale."

Chapter Seven

BY one p.m. that day the police had interviewed and taken statements from all the people in the house, and Gunderson gave permission for everybody who so wanted to leave. Most wasted no time.

Jessica decided to start back to Manhattan immediately after lunch. Preston was upset and anxious, waiting for the imminent descent of the media, and there could be no enjoyment left in the weekend. She felt a little guilty about leaving him in the lurch, but, in fact, he encouraged her to go.

"I'd like you away, out of it all," he said. "Come back again soon, when it's all over, and spend a truly restful weekend."

He was apologetic that he couldn't return with her; but as he explained, he felt he had to stay on hand for the time being. In spite of her assurance that she could perfectly well return to the city by train, he insisted on arranging for a limousine and chauffeur.

"You arrived in style; you'll go back the same way," he said firmly.

He came outside and kissed her gently on the cheek. "Safe trip," he said. He waved her off as the car bowled down the drive.

In the back Jessica settled down to chew over the possibilities of her embryonic plot. However, just as the car reached the end of the driveway and was about to turn onto the road, a figure with his hand raised stepped out from behind a tree. The driver hesitated.

"It's all right," Jessica said, "do stop. I know the gentleman."

It was Roy Gunderson. He opened the rear door. "Would you mind dropping me at police headquarters, ma'am?"

"Delighted, Mr. Gunderson."

He climbed in and the car moved off.

"How strange you haven't an official car available," Jessica said dryly.

He grunted. "Can we talk?"

"By all means."

Gunderson closed the partition behind the driver, then sank back into the deep seat. "I want to know about your problem," he said.

"Problem? I don't know . . ."

"You've had a look on your face, Mrs. Fletcher. Somethin's worrying you—somethin' about this case. I want to know what it is."

Jessica shook her head firmly. "No, Mr. Gunderson, this is really none of my business."

"I'd like to make it your business. You see, I figure this is a screwy sort of crime, like in a book. Not the usual sort of thing we have to handle. Now, seems to me you have the sort of brain . . ."

"The *screwy* sort of brain, do you mean?"

"The, let's say, ingenious sort of brain that could see to the bottom of this mystery."

"It's kind of you to say so, but I'm sure that's not true.

You think I know something that I haven't told you. I assure you I don't.''

"I'd like to tell you some of the things I learned this morning," Gunderson continued, "particularly what McCallum had to say."

"Should you do that?"

"Why not? Cops talk to each other about what they're told. And sometimes to outside experts they think can help. Let's call you one of those. Want to hear?"

Jessica gave a little chuckle. "Mr. Gunderson, you know quite well I do."

"So, there it is," Gunderson finished. "What d'you think?"

"Dear me, it's all extremely interesting, isn't it?"

"Any . . . observations?"

"Not just at the moment. I'd like to mull it over for a while first."

"You goin' to tell me now what's on your mind?"

"It's nothing specific, just vague ideas. There's only one definite point that occurs to me."

"What's that?"

"Well, someone killed Sherlock Holmes."

"That New York gumshoe was no Sherlock Holmes."

"Ah, but he was, Chief. At least, he was at the moment he was killed. The question is: did the killer know he was?"

Gunderson narrowed his eyes. "What?"

Jessica took a deep breath. "At first you thought you were investigating the murder of Captain McCallum. You said you wanted to find a motive. Then the Captain turned up and you discovered the true identity of the victim. Now, quite obviously, you're going to be looking for somebody with a motive for killing Baxendale.''

"Of course.''

"Such a person might have followed him to New Holvang and have no connection with anybody at the party. Indeed, I hope that *is* the case.''

"So?''

"Well, we mustn't forget that it was the *Captain* who went to the party as Sherlock Holmes. Suppose the murderer didn't know Caleb had taken the outfit off?''

"You mean . . . thought he was shooting at McCallum? But the shooting was done from the front.''

"Yes, but it was night. There was probably only enough light for the killer to see that very distinctive cape and deerstalker.''

Gunderson frowned. "What you're telling me is that we have *two* possible intended victims—*two* sets of suspects—depending on who the killer thought he was killing.''

"I'm afraid so. And you can't afford to neglect either line of inquiry, can you?''

Gunderson sighed and stared disconsolately out of the window. "Mrs. Fletcher, between church and football and the fact that the town council never calls me, this is my favorite day of the week. Now you've just made it the worst Sunday I've spent in ten years.''

On arriving in New York, Jessica went straight to her hotel. She spent a quiet evening and went to bed early.

The next morning she awoke having come to a firm decision. She had just finished dressing, when there was a knock on the door. It was Grady. He was carrying a bundle of newspapers.

"Seen these?" he asked, after they'd greeted each other.

"No, are they very bad?"

He handed her a copy of the *Daily News*. The front page carried a blazing headline: BIZARRE MURDER STALKS POSH PARTY. Below, in slightly smaller type were the words: Society Detective Slain.

There was a photo of Preston's home, and one of Dexter Baxendale.

"I don't think I want to read all this," Jessica said.

"Just listen to this bit."

He took the paper back from her and ran his eye down the column. "Ah, here we are: 'McCallum had registered at the inn shortly after ten-thirty. The internationally known fast-food king was accompanied by a young woman whose identity has not yet been divulged by authorities.' "

"Oh, poor Louise," said Jessica.

"I suppose it had to come out eventually. By the way, you're mentioned, Aunt Jess."

"Oh no! Am I?"

"Relax. It only says, let me see, er . . . , 'Also present at the party were best-selling mystery novelist Jessica Fletcher and ex-Broadway composer Peter Brill.' " Grady chuckled. "Peter will just love that 'ex.' Oh, and something else rather funny: one of the other papers refers to you as *Mr*. J. B. Fletcher."

"That's fine. Fame is not for me. The fewer people who know about me, the better I'll be pleased. Which is why I'm going home today. In fact, now."

She crossed the room, picked up a suitcase, put it on the bed, and began packing.

"Yeah, I thought you might decide that," Grady said. "I

think it's a pity, though. I bet you could solve this case. You were the first to realize the body wasn't Caleb's.''

"I'm not a detective, Grady. I'm a substitute English teacher.''

"You mean a writer.''

"I don't know what I mean, but I do know that Ethel Jenks is leaving Wednesday to visit her daughter in Montpelier and I promised I'd take her class.''

"They can get somebody else.''

"The truth is, I want to go back. Maybe I'm old-fashioned, but I don't have much use for city life, and frankly, except for you and Kitt, I don't much care for the people either.''

"Including Preston Giles?'' he asked quietly.

Jessica looked at him for a moment, then carried on with her packing.

"At least you could have called and told him you were leaving.''

"I'll call him from Cabot Cove.'' She smiled. "You know, it's a bit unseemly for you to be fixing up your old auntie with a suitor, no matter how pleasant or distinguished he might be.''

"Hey, I wasn't. Honest.''

"Oh, but you were. Honest.''

He shrugged. "Well, I'm sorry you guys didn't hit it off.''

"But, my dear, that's the trouble.'' Jessica's voice was almost sad. "We were starting to hit it off much *too* well.''

She snapped shut her suitcase, then reached into her purse and took out a five-dollar bill. She was just putting it under the ashtray next to her bed when the phone rang.

"Answer that, will you, Grady?''

Grady did so, listened for a few seconds, then covered the

mouthpiece. "Somebody called Chris Landon—*New York Times*."

"Oh, tell them I've been forced to go home today. I'm starting for Cabot Cove within the hour. If they want to send somebody there to interview me, fine; but I can't possibly see them today."

Grady relayed the message and hung up. He looked at his watch.

"Sorry I can't come to the station and see you off, Aunt Jess, but I must get to the office."

"Of course you must."

Jessica moved to him and gave him a big hug. "Take care of yourself, dear. My love to Kitt, and my thanks to her for making last week almost tolerable. Bring her up to Cabot Cove soon. Promise?"

"I promise, Aunt Jess," Grady said.

Half an hour later Jessica was walking along the platform of the railway station, about to board the train, when she suddenly heard a voice calling frantically from behind her.

"Mrs. Fletcher! Aunt Jess!"

She turned her head in surprise. Dashing toward her was Kitt.

Jessica stopped and stared as the girl came running up. She caught at Jessica's arm and stood panting, trying to get her breath.

"My dear, what on earth's the matter?" Jessica exclaimed.

Kitt gulped down a big mouthful of air. "Oh, Aunt Jess—it's Grady."

A cold hand clutched at Jessica's heart. She felt herself go white.

"What about him?" she whispered.

"He's been arrested!"

"What?"

"On suspicion of murder."

They gazed speechlessly at each other.

Chapter Eight

"CHIEF Gunderson," Jessica said forcefully, "my nephew did *not* kill that private detective."

Gunderson fumbled for matches and relit his cigar. "I sure hope you're right, Mrs. Fletcher. He seems like a nice young man—for a thief."

"Thief?" Jessica was indignant. "What *are* you talking about?"

"Fact is, Mrs. Fletcher, he's been stealing confidential information from his company."

"I don't believe it!"

Gunderson shrugged. "I wouldn't expect you to, ma'am, but right now he's being questioned by county detectives who aren't so sure."

Jessica threw up her hands in exasperation.

They were in a New York City precinct station. She had rushed straight there as soon as Kitt had explained where Grady was being held. But she hadn't yet been able to see him. Kitt herself had gone to phone Preston.

"County detectives?" Jessica said. "Why aren't *you* questioning him, Mr. Gunderson?"

"Matter of jurisdiction. When it comes to murder, tne

county cops have a way of taking over. Guess they figure a small-town chief like me is in over his head."

"If you believe Grady is guilty, they may be right."

The muscles around Gunderson's mouth tightened for a moment. Then, as he looked at Jessica, and perhaps sensed the anguish she was feeling, he softened his manner.

He crossed the sparsely furnished room, pulled out a chair, and sat down opposite her.

"Look, Mrs. Fletcher, I know how you feel. I realize he's kin. But listen to the facts."

He took his cigar from his mouth. "At daybreak this morning we found Baxendale's car parked a half mile from the Giles place. In the glove compartment there was a confidential real estate report belonging to Caleb McCallum. We've checked with him, and he tells us it must have been taken from his office sometime Friday morning."

"But why do you assume the thief was Grady?"

"He had access, ma'am."

"So, I'm sure, did many other employees."

"Not too many. Half a dozen, according to McCallum."

"Miss Vickers among them, I assume."

"Yes. And she's being questioned this very minute. Remember, however, Baxendale was discovered in your nephew's room."

"But assuming for a moment that Grady did take it, he would never have been so crazy as to carry it around with him—right out to New Holvang—and then leave it unguarded in his room."

"He might have. Could be he was about to hand it over to somebody, somebody who was going to contact him, though he didn't know just where or when. But he had to have the report handy. He'd figure it was safe enough. If the report wasn't missed and no hue and cry started, he could reasonably assume the theft wouldn't be discovered until this morning—by which time he would have gotten rid of the report. As he would have done if things had gone according to plan. And it wouldn't even matter if anybody—'cept McCallum himself—happened to see the report in his room. To a servant, for example, it'd just be business papers, which they'd assume your nephew had a perfect right to have.''

Jessica considered this. Things were not looking good for Grady. ''Chief Gunderson, I don't want to cast undue suspicion, but all you've said applies equally to Ashley Vickers.''

''Except for one thing: there's no evidence that Baxendale was ever in Miss Vickers' room; it would be much more dangerous for her to keep the report there—because she might well expect McCallum himself to visit her.''

''I don't agree,'' Jessica said. ''I heard her say that for several months her relationship with the Captain had been a purely business one.''

''Well, she would say that, wouldn't she—once she discovered McCallum had found another playmate in Little Red Riding Hood? But I don't figure she found *that* out until late Saturday night. Don't forget, either, that *Mrs*. McCallum certainly thought there was something going on between her husband and Vickers.''

Jessica didn't say anything. Gunderson seemed to be warming to his task. He took a puff on his cigar, then went on:

''However, say Vickers was telling the truth. Fact remains, McCallum brought her with him for some reason. Say it was just business. Or again, McCallum knew one of his employees was leaking information. Suppose he suspected Vickers and wanted to keep an eye on her. She wouldn't realize his motive. But whatever his reason for having her along, she must have thought there was a good chance McCallum would be in and out of her room. It would have been a risk to have the report there. Oh, I know none of this is conclusive. But the truth is that the evidence against her is not so strong as against your nephew.''

Jessica sighed. ''Grady himself raised the alarm when he saw someone in his room . . .''

'' 'Course he did. And if he had that report hidden there, it'd explain why he got so steamed up when he saw the beam of that flashlight bobbing about.''

''That's nonsense. If he'd had anything incriminating in his room, he wouldn't have drawn attention to the intruder. He would have made an excuse to Miss Donovan, then hurried quietly up the back stairs. He'd never have come charging through the living room the way he did, letting Kitt tell us all what was going on.''

''He panicked.''

''He's not the panicking sort. And his manner was not that of a guilty person. At the party he was very relaxed and rather pleased with himself.''

''So you say, Mrs. Fletcher. But I'm afraid your nephew's manner is not evidence.''

''All right,'' Jessica asked suddenly, ''answer me this: how did the papers get to Baxendale's car?''

''What do you mean?''

''Well, according to your theory, when Grady took Baxendale downstairs to see him off the premises, he knew there was a chance Baxendale had found the report and had it on him. Are you telling me that, with a possible jail sentence staring him in the face, Grady just let him walk off without searching him?''

"Could be he tried."

"What do you mean?"

"Your nephew got the better of Baxendale once. But he might not have a second time. Baxendale was a pro. He'd be on his guard. Say your nephew demanded that Baxendale turn out his pockets, Baxendale refused, they fought—and this time Baxendale won. He got away, took the report back to his car, locked it in safely. Then it occurred to him: why turn in your nephew to McCallum? Why not seek a partnership? Your nephew knew where the report could be sold, so Baxendale would need him. He goes back to the house again, sees your nephew a second time, and starts to apply the pressure—let him in for fifty percent, or he turns your nephew over to McCallum. Your nephew sees red, and bang . . ."

Jessica tried another tack. "If this leaking of information has been going on for some time, whoever's responsible will have made a good sum of money already. I know the state of Grady's bank account: anemic."

"Naturally he wouldn't put the dough in his regular account. And incidentally, neither would Ashley Vickers. But we're looking into it, all the same."

Jessica looked up. "Fingerprints," she said abruptly. "If Grady had been handling that report, his prints would be all over it."

"We checked. Prints are all smudged."

Jessica got to her feet. "Nothing I can say will shake you, will it?"

"I got an open mind, Mrs. Fletcher. But I gotta go by the facts. Bring me some facts, something solid in Grady's favor—or something solid against another person—and I'll be pleased to shake hands with your nephew and tell him I'm sorry. But until then . . ."

When Jessica went outside she found an anxiety-stricken Kitt awaiting her.

"Well?" the girl asked eagerly.

Jessica shook her head. "He's got an answer for everything, my dear. He's built up quite a formidable case, even if it is purely circumstantial."

Kitt took her by the arm. "Well, I have some good news. I got through to Mr. Giles. He was terribly shocked. He said he'd call his lawyer friend, Karl Teretsky, to get Grady released on bail today."

"Oh, thank heavens. Karl Teretsky? I've heard of him. He's very expensive, isn't he?"

"One of the most expensive in New York, but one of the best. And Mr. Giles is coming straight here himself."

"Oh, good." Jessica gave a wry smile. "Not, I suppose that there's a lot he can do. But just having him here will help."

By early afternoon Grady had been released and Preston had arrived hotfoot from New Holvang. He, Grady, and Teretsky had a hurried conference; then Teretsky went off to put some inquiries in motion.

Preston, Grady, Jessica, and Kitt went for a late lunch at a small Italian restaurant across from the police station.

At the close of the meal Preston slipped away to phone Teretsky. He came back looking a little grim.

"Well, things aren't really any better, I'm afraid," he said. "It seems Baxendale *did* have a reputation as a blackmailer—which supports the police theory about his attempt to pressure Grady."

Grady gave a groan. "I'm sick of saying it! I never saw that report. And I didn't set eyes on Baxendale again. I took him downstairs and saw him off the premises. That was that."

Jessica tapped his hand. "*We* know that, dear, but we must look at it from the police viewpoint."

"I know," he sighed.

"There's one thing," Jessica said slowly, "that I should have raised with the chief: the Sherlock Holmes costume. Why was Baxendale wearing it?"

"I mentioned that to Karl," Preston said. "The cops just figure he slipped back to the party and took it out of the front closet as a sort of disguise so he could mingle with the guests. At least it would cover his hair and that very expensive suit."

"Oh, that's fiddle-faddle, Preston," Jessica said impatiently. "Baxendale wasn't a mind reader. How could he possibly have known the costume was in the closet? Anyway, why should he want to mingle? If he had been meaning to blackmail Grady, all he had to do was phone the house, ask to speak to him, and demand that Grady come outside to meet him. To wander around the house looking for him, knowing he might run into you or me or Kitt, would have been crazy."

"Even so," Grady said, "there must be a reason he was dressed that way."

Kitt spoke up suddenly. "Perhaps Captain Caleb gave him the costume, or told him where it was, and asked him to put it on."

"What reason would he give?"

"As the police think: so he could mingle easier. But not to look for you."

"I don't get it."

"Afraid I don't, either," Preston put in.

"Look: Caleb was going off with Little Red Riding

Hood. Baxendale was working for him, but still hadn't found the report. He needed to go on searching. Or perhaps keep somebody under surveillance. He needed a disguise to do so. Say he phoned McCallum, told him he'd been rumbled and evicted, and wanted to get back indoors. So McCallum *didn't,* as he says, put the costume in the closet, but took it out and left it somewhere on the grounds for Baxendale to find.''

Grady said thoughtfully: "Well, it's logical up to a point. Trouble is, that costume just wasn't a very effective disguise—not in bright lighting, indoors. From behind, for a few seconds, okay—but people would only have to get a glimpse of his face . . .''

"With most of the guests that wouldn't matter," Jessica said.

"It wouldn't if Caleb hadn't been wearing the costume all evening. I mean, can't you imagine people going up to Baxendale, momentarily thinking he was McCallum? 'Oh, have you and Caleb changed costumes?' Or: 'I didn't know there were two Sherlock Holmeses here.' No, that costume would have been useless as a disguise; it would only have drawn attention to him. Don't you agree, Aunt Jess?''

But Jessica had stopped listening. She had just seen a familiar figure enter the restaurant and hurry across to a wall phone.

"Look who's here," she murmured.

"Ashley Vickers," Grady said slowly. "So she's been released too." He grinned wryly. "I honestly don't know whether to be glad or sorry.''

"Excuse me a moment," Jessica said.

She rose and moved slowly across the restaurant toward the phone. Ashley got a number and Jessica waited while

95

she talked urgently for a few seconds, then hung up. Jessica moved to her as she turned.

Ashley raised her eyebrows. "Mrs. Fletcher. What are you doing here?"

Jessica nodded her head, indicating the group seated across the room.

"I think it's called a war council. Would you like to join us?"

"Thanks, but no," Ashley said. "I've just spent several hours being hounded by two homicide detectives, and all I want now is a hot bath and a cold drink."

She started to move. Jessica put a hand on her arm.

"Ashley, often there is strength in numbers. You know the police are convinced that either you or my nephew murdered that private detective."

"But that's not true," Ashley said sharply.

Jessica frowned. "What do you mean?"

"Didn't you know? They've pinpointed the time of death. Preston's neighbors heard a loud noise at eleven-fifteen. They thought it was a sonic boom, so they didn't investigate. The police checked. There were no jets overhead Saturday night. That sonic boom was the sound of the shotgun."

Jessica cast her mind back. "Eleven-fifteen . . ."

"Yes," said Ashley, "a time for which I could gratefully provide them with an ironclad alibi."

"Oh, was that when . . . ?"

"Right. At eleven-fifteen I was sitting half-naked in an upstairs bedroom while *you* were washing my dress out. So I'm afraid that leaves Grady as the one and only suspect. Excuse me."

She walked away.

Thoughtfully Jessica went back to her table. She relayed

Ashley's news. Grady and Preston looked grim, but Kitt said excitedly:

"Eleven-fifteen! But that's wonderful! Grady and I were together at that time."

Preston said gently: "My dear Kitt, I'm afraid that's like Bonnie Parker alibiing Clyde Barrow."

Her face fell. "Oh yes, I suppose so."

Suddenly Grady sprang to his feet. "I'm going back to the office."

They stared at him. "Today?" Jessica said.

"Why not? I have to do something or I'll go crazy. I can usually manage to lose myself in figures."

"But won't you mind showing yourself?" asked Kitt. "Everybody there will be sure to know . . ."

"So what? I've done nothing to be ashamed of. I want McCallum to know that. And I have to face the others sometime."

"You won't find Caleb at the office this afternoon," Preston said. "He told me he'd be spending the day on his yacht at Bayside."

Grady shrugged. "Just as long as he knows sometime."

They left the restaurant. Grady and Kitt went off together. Preston hailed a taxi. He and Jessica got in, and he gave the driver the address of Coventry House.

There was a companionable silence for a moment or two. Then Preston said quietly: "Worried?"

"I can't help it."

"I know. But cheer up. Karl Teretsky is the best trial lawyer in the state."

"Will it come to that, Preston? A trial?"

He shook his head. "I don't suppose so for a moment."

Then he took her hand and spoke gravely. "Jess, you have my word: Grady will be exonerated."

"Thank you, Preston. I know you're trying."

He looked at her a little sadly for a moment. "Kitt tells me she caught up with you at Grand Central."

Jessica looked awkward. "I was going to call you, Preston, I give you my word."

"From Maine." He looked out of the window. "I feel somewhat foolish. This weekend—before the trouble—was the happiest time I'd spent in years." He looked at her. "Did I misread you so badly?"

Jessica hesitated. "Of course not. But back home we have a saying: flowers that bloom too quickly are fair game for a late frost."

Preston looked amused. "Do you really say that?"

"Actually, no." Jessica smiled.

They both laughed. "That's better," he said, and squeezed her hand.

"You will be going home then?"

She shook her head decidedly. "Oh, not now. Not until I know that Grady is all right."

A minute or so later the taxi drew up outside Preston's office. He got out, then turned around. "Dinner tonight?" he asked.

"Well," Jessica replied, "there's a lot to do . . ."

"But you do have to eat. Why not with me?"

Jessica smiled. "All right, I'd love to. Thank you."

"Great. I'll call you later."

He took a twenty-dollar bill from his pocket and handed it to the driver. "Take the lady to her hotel." He gave a wave and was gone.

Jessica stared after him absently for a moment, then started to rummage vigorously in her purse. She was recalled to reality by the cabdriver. "Lady, which hotel?" he asked in a tone of superhuman patience.

"Oh, I'm sorry," Jessica said, "I was thinking of something else. No, I've changed my mind. Driver, do you know a place called—now dear me, where is it? Bayview? Baytown?"

"We got a Bay Ridge, lady. That's in Brooklyn. In Jersey you got your Bayonne. Out on the Island, you got your Bay Shore, your Bayville, your Bayside . . ."

Jessica snapped her fingers. "That's it! Bayside! The Bayside Yacht Club. Would you please drive me there?"

The driver held up Preston's twenty-dollar bill. "Won't get there on this, lady."

"Oh, I'm prepared to pay the difference, naturally."

The driver turned right around in his seat. "Listen, lady, to tell you the truth, I wanna get home. My feet are killing me. Yeah—I know—a guy in my job should have problems somewhere else, but with me it's my feet. Some joke, huh?"

"Oh, it's no joke. My friend Lena Miller had an awful time for years. She had these little calluses—like corns, only they're not corns . . ."

The driver's face lit up as though he had met an old friend.

"Say, that's what *I* got!"

"Really? Then we're going to have to get you some ointment."

"Naw, I've tried all that stuff."

"Not *all* that stuff, you haven't. Back home, we make some ourselves. Very secret."

"You're kidding. You know, my old man's got the same problem. I think it's heretical."

"I think you're very probably right," Jessica said gravely.

"This ointment stuff—it does the trick?"

"It cured Lena Miller."

"That so? Gee, this I gotta try. How can I get hold of some?"

"Well, if you like I can tell you how to make it. Or write it out for you."

"Aw, would you do that?"

"Certainly, but it's quite complicated. It'll take some time. So, if you'd like to drive on . . ."

"You win, lady. For something that'd fix my feet, I'd drive to California."

He faced front again, and the cab pulled away from the curb.

Jessica took out her notebook. "I'll explain what I'm writing," she said. "Now, this is how we make it . . ."

Chapter Nine

WHEN the taxi drew up at the Bayside Yacht Club, the meter read thirty-three dollars and eighty cents.

Jessica looked up from her purse in dismay. "Oh dear," she said, "how awful."

"You can't make it?"

"I'm sorry, Bernie, I was sure I'd brought more cash with me. I don't suppose you'd take a credit card, would you? No, I didn't think so."

He gazed at her indulgently. "Look, Mrs. Fletcher, you gonna be here long?"

"Well, I can't be sure. But not if I can help it."

"Okay, then, I'll wait for you and drive you back to the city off the meter."

"Oh, Bernie, I couldn't ask you to do that."

"What you gonna do—take the subway? Forget it. Go do what you're gonna do."

Jessica stared at him. "Do you know something, Bernie?"

"I don't know nothing."

"All the same, you've taught me a valuable lesson."

"That so? What?"

"That there are some very kind people in New York."

" 'Course there are."

"In fact, probably just as many as there are anywhere else. They just take a bit of digging for." She got out. "I'll be as quick as I can."

"No rush. It's peaceful here. I got my paper and the radio. And your secret recipe." He held up some pages torn from her notebook.

It didn't take Jessica long to locate McCallum's boat, the *Chowder King*. It was one of the largest yachts berthed at the Bayside Yacht Club.

As she walked along the wharf, she spotted the familiar figure of McCallum, hosing down the deck.

"Hullo?" she called out. "*Chowder King* ahoy! Captain Caleb."

He spun around. His expression was momentarily grim. Then he recognized her and made an effort to smile.

"Mrs. Fletcher. What a surprise. A delightful one, of course."

"I hope you don't mind my coming," Jessica said.

"Not at all. Come aboard."

He stopped the hose and dropped it on the deck. She climbed the short gangplank and he assisted her off it.

"Thank you, Captain."

"What can I do for you, Mrs. Fletcher? I assume this isn't just a social call."

"Unfortunately not. Captain, you know, of course, that Grady was arrested this morning."

He gave a shrug. "The evidence is conclusive, I'm afraid."

"The evidence is far from conclusive, Mr. McCallum. It's wholly circumstantial."

"Circumstantial evidence can be as strong as any other kind."

"I suppose you've been talking to Chief Gunderson," Jessica said.

"Thankfully, no. Gunderson is an incompetent fool. He's a political hack, putting in time till his pension comes. However, in this case he does have his facts straight."

He turned away, took a mop out of a bucket that was standing nearby, and started to swab the deck with it.

Oh no, Jessica thought, you're not going to get rid of me as easily as that.

She looked around and spotted a canvas and aluminum chair near the rail. She walked across to it, carried it to the center of the deck, and sat firmly down in it.

"What facts are those, Mr. McCallum?" she asked.

He stopped swabbing and stared at her for a few seconds. Then he straightened up. "All right, I'll tell you. Can't do any harm."

He walked across and stood in front of her, resting his hands on the handle of the mop.

"Someone in my organization has been stealing information on proposed sites for my Chowder Houses. Those leaks have cost me a great deal of money."

"Yes, I'm aware of that."

"I hired Dexter Baxendale to ferret out the guilty party. He eventually narrowed the list down to six possible culprits."

"Among whom no doubt was Grady?"

"Right."

"And Miss Vickers?"

McCallum's eyes narrowed. "She was a theoretical possibility. I don't know if you'd care for the names of the other four?''

"Not at this stage, thank you," Jessica said seriously. "They wouldn't mean anything to me. Please go on."

"At Baxendale's suggestion I made those six people— and only those six—aware of a confidential real estate report I had just received. The contents of it could be worth big, big money to someone if I acted on it. Of course, if the information did leak out, I didn't have to. I let it be thought, though, that I *was* going to act on the information. Today."

"I see. Your object in this being to force your traitor to act quickly."

"Yeah. He or she'd have to steal the report on Friday and dispose of it over the weekend."

"And it *was* stolen on Friday?"

"That's right. But I still didn't know who by."

Resisting the impulse to correct him with an admonitory *by whom*, Jessica asked, "Wasn't that rather careless? Wouldn't it have been preferable to leave the report somewhere in your office, apparently unguarded, but with Mr. Baxendale watching covertly to see who took it?"

McCallum looked embarrassed. "Well, that was the original idea. But there was a foul-up. Baxendale, the fool, left his post for five minutes, and in that time the report vanished."

"Dear me," Jessica said, "now that seems to me rather suspicious. Didn't it occur to you that Baxendale might have been in, er, cahoots with the traitor and have deliberately left his post for five minutes?"

McCallum scowled. "It crossed my mind," he admitted. "But he convinced me it was a genuine mistake. Besides, at that stage I had no choice but to trust him. There wasn't time to call in another detective agency. So I didn't let it be known I'd discovered the theft, and Baxendale arranged, at no extra charge, for all five suspects to be closely watched over the weekend by himself and his operatives . . ."

Jessica interrupted. "Five suspects? I thought you said six . . ." She broke off. "Oh, I see. You yourself were going to keep an eye on Miss Vickers, I presume."

"Nothing of the sort," he snapped.

"No? Then may I ask why in fact you invited her to Preston's house with you?"

"That's my business, I reckon, Mrs. Fletcher."

"I think not, Mr. McCallum. Not when my nephew is facing a murder trial. However, I won't press the point. You were saying the five other suspects were put under surveillance . . . ?"

"That's right. From the moment they left the office."

"Really? That means somebody must have followed Grady to Grand Central when he caught up with me there?"

"I guess so."

"How interesting," Jessica said thoughtfully. "I've never been kept under surveillance by a detective before. At least, not as far as I know." She gave a sudden decisive nod. "Yes, of course! It would have been that big burly man with the brown hair."

McCallum looked startled. "You spotted him?"

"Well," Jessica said, "naturally, I couldn't be absolutely *sure* . . ."

A point to me, she thought, with satisfaction. Definitely cheating, of course. But among Baxendale's operatives there was almost certain to have been one who was big, burly, and brown-haired; and no one could ever *prove* she hadn't spotted him.

Without giving McCallum a chance to work this out, she went on quickly. "So you knew Grady was being watched at the party on Saturday night?"

"I sure hoped he was."

"You suspected from the start he was the culprit?"

"No. He's one of my brightest boys. But I wanted to be sure it wasn't him. Naturally, when Louise and I accepted Press' invitation, we had no idea your nephew was going to show up there."

Jessica furrowed her brow. "But I'm puzzled. You believed Grady was being watched. Yet when you were told by Chief Gunderson that Baxendale had been in the house that night, you were apparently surprised."

"That Gunderson's sure got a big mouth," McCallum said disgustedly. "But it's true. I *was* surprised. I didn't know Baxendale was tailing your nephew *personally*. I figured that one of the guests in fancy dress was a Baxendale operative. I still do. My bet is that Baxendale came along late, knew your nephew was safely under surveillance downstairs, and decided to search his room. Where he found the report. 'Course, he didn't know your nephew was outside the house and would see his flashlight. So he was caught."

"And why didn't he produce the report then and expose Grady?"

McCallum shrugged. "Probably because he had no proof where he'd found it. But we know he found it somewhere—it was discovered later in his car—and we know he had been in your nephew's room. The inference is obvious."

"Do you really think so? Then explain to me why the document was found in Baxendale's car. Why walk half a mile, lock the report in his car, and come back to the house? Why didn't he bring the report to you? He did know you were there, I suppose. You did tell him where he could contact you over the weekend?"

"Naturally I did. Look, Mrs. Fletcher, I'm not denying Baxendale was a crook—had decided to double-cross me and perhaps sell the report himself. It's possible—probable, even. But it doesn't alter the situation regarding your nephew. And if it is true—well, Baxendale sure paid the penalty."

Jessica nodded. "Yes, he did, didn't he?"

Something in her tone angered McCallum. "What d'you mean by that?" he asked hotly.

"Just that I don't think you'd take kindly to being double-crossed, Mr. McCallum. You'd get very angry with anyone who tried."

He flushed. "You saying I killed Baxendale?"

"Merely that you had means and motive—just as strong a motive as Grady, in fact—even admitting he was the thief, which, of course, I don't."

"I also have an alibi, Mrs. Fletcher."

"Ah yes, the young, er, lady in the Red Riding Hood costume. So does Grady. Quite as good a one, if not better. I mean, granted that Grady and Kitt are very fond of each other, so she could perhaps be expected to lie for him—well, so are you and Little Red Riding Hood fond of each other. After all, you couldn't resist the temptation to go off with her when Louise's departure gave you the opportunity. That left Miss Vickers unwatched and with a wonderful chance to get rid of that report."

"I never seriously suspected Ashley. Besides, the cops have cleared her. They called to tell me. You yourself give her an alibi for the time of the murder."

"Yes," said Jessica, "for the time of the *murder.*"

"Well, there you are. Now, Mrs. Fletcher, you must excuse me. I have lots to do."

"Oh, certainly, I'll go."

Jessica stood up and moved toward the rail. "You know, Mr. McCallum," she said pleasantly, "there's one thing we may be forgetting: how can we be sure *anyone* intended to kill Baxendale? With him wearing that Sherlock Holmes costume, the killer may have been after you."

He shook his head. "Not a chance. The police say the shot was fired from no more than fifteen feet away."

"I just can't help thinking: it was such a dark, cloudy night. And you know, if a mistake *was* made . . ." She broke off. "Oh well, you're probably right." But she sounded far from convinced.

"Mrs. Fletcher, you're a pretty shrewd cookie," McCallum said, "but you're scratching up the wrong tree. You see, nobody has a motive to kill me. My employees know full well that I *am* Cap'n Caleb's Chowder Houses. Without me, it all falls apart. As for my wife, Louise—we have a prenuptial agreement. While I'm alive, she lives like a queen. If I die, she gets almost nothing." He smiled. "So much for your theory of mistaken identity."

Jessica put her foot on the gangplank. "But on the basis of that, can you really say *nobody* has a motive to kill you? I don't think *I* could be so confident. There is such a thing as pure hatred, you know."

She started down the gangplank, then paused and turned.

"All the same, I 'm glad you said none of your employees has a motive to kill you."

"Why?"

"Because if mistaken identity should be proven, I have your word for it that Grady didn't have a motive."

"If he's still technically an employee of mine, he won't be for long."

"Technically? But he's at his desk at McCallum Enterprises this afternoon."

The Captain's face darkened. "You mean he had the colossal nerve to go to work today?"

"Why not? He's done nothing wrong. And that's something I know. I appreciate your hospitality, Captain Caleb. And no thank you, I *won't* have a drink."

Jessica stepped off the gangplank, turned, gave him a cheerful little wave, and tripped away along the wharf.

It was late afternoon when Jessica got back to her hotel. She went up to her room and immediately telephoned Grady. He answered almost at once.

"Grady?"

"Oh, hullo, Aunt Jess."

"How did it go at the office?"

"Not too bad. I got a few fishy looks, and one or two people kept their distance. I felt like the guy who uses the wrong toothpaste."

"Well, I think you were very brave to go. Grady, what time does the office close?"

"What's it matter?"

"What time, Grady?"

"Six-thirty, seven. Why?"

"That real estate report . . ."

"Oh, Lord, am I tired of that report!"

"Listen, Grady, this is important. Baxendale found it at Preston's house. The only two employees who could have brought it there were you and Ashley. That automatically eliminates the other four suspects. We know it wasn't you . . ."

"Thanks," he said dryly. "Sometimes I'm beginning to have doubts even about that."

"Be serious, Grady. Ashley had to be the culprit. You agree on that?"

"Yes, I suppose so," he said somewhat reluctantly.

"Then we have to prove it."

"But how on earth . . ."

"I want to look around her office," Jessica interrupted.

He drew his breath in sharply. "Aunt Jess, that's police business."

"At the moment, my dear, the police seem to be making it their business to convict you of murder."

"But if you were caught . . ."

"I don't think I'd face a very severe sentence, not as a first offender. But anyway, I shall take great care not to be. Of course, I'll need your help."

"I don't like it."

"Grady, you must trust me. I'm going to get you out of this. You would never have been at that party if it hadn't been for me."

"Well, *you'd* never have been there if it hadn't been for *me*. I submitted your book to Coventry House, remember."

"If it comes to that, I introduced your father and mother to each other, so you wouldn't *be* if it weren't for me. However, this is pointless. Now, will you cooperate?"

Grady gave a sigh. "I suppose, as there's obviously no way I'm going to talk you out of this, I'll have to. When were you thinking of mounting this expedition?"

"Tonight. Can you pick me up here at the hotel in"—she looked at her watch—"about an hour?"

"All right, if you're set on it. They can tack breaking and entering onto my murder-one sentence."

"Think positive, my boy. See you in an hour."

Jessica put down the receiver. That had been quickly settled. Fortunately. One of the reasons she had been so firm was that if she'd let him argue for long, he'd have talked her out of the project.

Almost as soon as she hung up, her phone rang. It was Preston.

"Where have you been?" he asked. "I've tried several times to get you, but the clerk said you hadn't been back since lunch. I was getting worried."

"I'm sorry, Preston. I went to see someone. I forgot you said you'd call."

"Oh, that's okay. Look, about tonight: I know a little restaurant . . ."

"Preston, do you mind if we keep options open for tonight? I may not be able to make it—or only rather late."

There was silence, and when he spoke she could hear the disappointment in his voice.

"No, of course, that's all right. If there's a chance of your having another dinner engagement . . ."

"It's nothing like that, I assure you. It's just I have a job to do. If you don't mind possibly wasting an evening, call me here later, about nine o'clock."

* * *

"Listen, Aunt Jess," Grady was saying, "Ashley may have taken those papers, but you know yourself she couldn't have killed Baxendale."

"Agreed. But her accomplice could have."

The two were in Grady's car, en route to McCallum Enterprises. Grady glanced briefly at her. "What accomplice?"

"I don't know. But she not only stole that report, but actually took it with her to New Holvang. Why?"

"Obviously to pass on to someone . . ." He broke off. "Oh, you mean to someone at the party?"

Jessica shrugged. "Well, that certainly seems most likely. It's clear she had to dispose of the report on Saturday or Sunday. Knowing that, she took the report with her to Preston's house—in spite of the risk involved. She must have had an arrangement with someone to hand it over. And remember: that someone was just as vulnerable as she was—and just as likely to commit murder."

Grady nodded thoughtfully. "Yes, it makes sense. But, Aunt Jess, it doesn't figure from any of this that Ashley would keep anything incriminating in her office."

"I realize that. But we'll never know unless we look. And there has to be something incriminating somewhere. It may be in her apartment."

Jessica paused and a very determined expression came over her face. "Tonight may be the first of several expeditions we have to make."

Ten minutes later Grady and Jessica entered the lobby of the McCallum Enterprises building. It was deserted, save for a uniformed security guard sitting at his desk. He looked at them with some surprise as they approached.

Trying to mask his nervousness, Grady said cheerily, "Evening, Tom."

"Evening, Mr. Fletcher. Working late tonight?"

"No. I just want to show my aunt where I work. She's visiting from Maine."

The guard nodded. "How do, ma'am. Hope you're enjoying your stay."

"Oh, it's been a rare experience, believe me," Jessica said.

"Anybody else around?" Grady asked casually.

"No, sir, you'll have it to yourself."

Grady nodded, took Jessica's arm, and escorted her toward the elevators, pointing like a tour guide to various extremely uninteresting objects as he did so.

They entered an elevator, Grady pressed a button, and the doors closed. They both breathed a sigh of relief as the elevator started to ascend.

"First obstacle cleared," he muttered.

"Now, when we get there," Jessica said, "I'm going to search Ashley's office. I want you to check the sales records."

He stared at her. "What?"

"We need to know the names of the people from whom the company bought the properties. Can you get them?"

He ran his fingers through his hair. "I guess so. They'll be in the computer."

"Good. Whoever bought and then resold those overpriced properties has to have some connection to Ashley—or to her contact."

The elevator stopped and the doors opened with a chime. Grady and Jessica stepped cautiously out, glancing both ways along a carpeted, dimly lit corridor.

Grady pointed and put his mouth close to Jessica's ear.

"Ashley's office is at the end of the corridor. Her name's on the door."

"Why are you whispering?" Jessica asked brightly.

"*Quiet!*" he hissed.

"Grady, for heaven's sake, there's no one to hear you. Now, off to your computer. Scoot!"

"All right, but it may take a while."

They went their separate ways.

The door of Ashley's office was open. Jessica slipped in. The lights of the city outside a huge glass panoramic window provided just enough illumination. She looked around for a few seconds, then moved quickly to Ashley's desk. She flipped on a desk light and sat down. Then she started to go through the drawers of the desk.

Five minutes later she sat back in disappointment. Nothing. Nothing but completely innocuous business papers.

However, one drawer was locked.

Jessica eyed it speculatively. In that drawer might be pay dirt. On the other hand, quite possibly it contained papers that were just normally confidential.

It was while these thoughts were flashing through Jessica's mind that she heard a faint sound. She jerked her head up. What was it? The next second she knew.

It was the whir of the elevator ascending.

Jessica froze. Then, like lightning, she switched off the desk lamp and flitted silently to the door. She peered cautiously along the corridor toward the elevators at the far end.

She told herself there was no need for alarm. Hundreds of people were employed in this building. Obviously, some of them worked late. There was no reason to assume that any-body would come near this office.

Jessica heard a chime. The doors slid back. There was an agonizing moment of suspense during which nothing happened. And then out of the elevator stepped Ashley Vickers.

Chapter Ten

JESSICA gave a muted gasp of horror, and her head shot back into the office like a tortoise withdrawing into its shell. Her mind whirled.

She was virtually certain Ashley had not seen her, because as the girl had stepped from the elevator, she was in the act of studying her face in a compact mirror.

But she would certainly be here within sixty seconds.

Jessica gazed around the room frantically.

There was no hiding place in the office. But there was one other door leading out of the room—set in the far wall. It was her only chance not to be caught in a highly embarrassing situation.

Almost willing the door not to be locked, Jessica darted across the room. She turned the knob and experienced a throb of relief as the door opened. She shot through it.

She found herself in a small private bathroom. She turned and pulled the door almost closed behind her, leaving it about an inch ajar—just enough to see through. There was a risk that Ashley would notice this and remember she had left the door closed. But if it enabled Jessica to see exactly what the girl was up to, it was a risk worth taking.

Jessica remained frozen, practically holding her breath,

one eye glued to the crack. She was unable to see the whole office, but had a clear view of the desk and a couple of filing cabinets.

What seemed like an age passed. Yet it could not have been more than half a minute before Jessica heard someone enter the room. The door to the corridor closed, and a second or two later Ashley came into her view.

The girl was carrying a purse, which she put down on the desk and opened. She fumbled inside it for a moment and took out a bunch of keys. She selected one, bent over the desk, and unlocked the one drawer Jessica had been unable to search.

Ashley reached in and took out a file folder. She then carefully removed a sheaf of papers from it. She folded these and put them in her purse. Next she closed the file and replaced it in the drawer, which she locked.

For several seconds Ashley stood quite still by the desk, staring at the floor as though in thought. At last she seemed to come to a decision. She raised her head and looked directly at the bathroom door.

She hesitated for a moment—and then started to walk straight toward it.

Jessica's heart missed a beat and she shrank back against the washbasin—desperately, but hopelessly, trying to think up some feasible explanation for her presence.

She heard Ashley's footsteps approaching. The door started to move.

It was at that moment that the telephone rang.

Jessica nearly jumped out of her skin. She heard Ashley give a little gasp.

There was an agonizing wait while the girl obviously stood, indecisive, her hand on the knob. Jessica held her breath, her fingernails pressed hard into the palms of her hands.

At last, Ashley retreated across the room. The next moment the telephone bell cut off sharply as she lifted the receiver. Her voice came—low, cautious.

"Yes?"

Then she audibly relaxed. "Oh, it's you. You scared me." Suddenly she sounded markedly annoyed. "Why are you calling me here?"

Ashley listened for a few seconds. "Well, I don't want you calling me *anywhere*. And yes, I *do* have it."

After a further short pause, she said angrily: "Talk? About what? I told you—after this, it's over. I won't have any part in murder."

Jessica smothered an involuntary gasp. She could hardly have hoped for anything as good as that. She strained her ears, trying to hear something—anything—of the voice on the other end. But she was too far away from the phone, even though Ashley's silence meant her caller must now be talking at length.

Eventually Ashley plainly cut in. "What, now? Tonight? No." After another wait she said: "All right, stop being hysterical. If it's that important, I suppose I can. Where are you?"

Ashley waited again, and Jessica imagined her jotting down an address. Sure enough, a moment later the girl said, "Got it," and Jessica heard the tearing of paper.

"I'll be there as soon as possible. But listen—they may be following me."

This time Ashley was silent for the longest period yet. "Well, all right," she finally said. Her voice sounded doubtful. "I'll do the best I can." Then came the sound of her replacing the receiver.

Once more Jessica waited, tense. Nonetheless, her apprehension of being discovered had now vanished. She would almost have welcomed a confrontation. That one word—*murder*—had changed the situation entirely.

However, a confrontation wasn't to be. Jessica again heard Ashley moving—this time away from the bathroom. The door to the corridor opened and closed. Then all was still.

Hastily Jessica emerged into the office. She badly wanted to sit down, get her breath, and collect her thoughts. But there was no time. She had to know who Ashley was going to meet.

She hurried to the corridor, opened the door, and peered out. Ashley was walking briskly toward the elevators.

Jessica waited until she had entered a car and descended before starting to run down the corridor herself. She got to the elevators, jabbed impatiently at a button, and looked around her. She had no idea where Grady had gone. She tried a sort of muted shout, like a stage whisper.

"Grady!"

But there was no response. She had no choice but to go without him.

Jessica waited, gnawing at her lip, watching the indicator showing Ashley's car approaching the ground floor. Then the doors of another elevator slid back. Jessica shot in and pressed the ground-floor button.

When the elevator reached the lobby and Jessica emerged, there was no sign of Ashley. But the security guard, Tom, was still at his desk, writing in a big book.

Jessica hurried across to him. As she did so, she opened her purse and took out the first object her fingers met, which happened to be a fountain pen.

The guard looked up as she reached him.

"Has a young lady just left?" she asked breathlessly.

"Yes, ma'am—Miss Vickers. I was just signing her out. She seemed in a hurry."

"You didn't see which way she went, did you?"

He shook his head.

Jessica held up her fountain pen. "She dropped this," she said mendaciously. "I wanted to give it back to her."

He stuck out his hand. "That's all right, ma'am. Leave it with me. I'll see she gets it in the morning."

"Oh, no," Jessica said hastily. "She may need it tonight. I'll just see if I can catch her."

She turned and almost ran to the doors.

The guard stared after her. "But, ma'am . . . it can't matter tonight. It's only a pen. Ma'am . . ."

But Jessica ignored him. The guard shook his head in disbelief and returned to his book.

Jessica emerged from the brightness of the lobby into the night and stood helpless and lost for a moment, peering up and down the street. There was still no sign of Ashley.

Then, miraculously, she spotted her quarry. At least . . . yes, it had to be. The girl in question was some distance away, and there was only street lighting to go by, but it was impossible to mistake that magnificent outline. Ashley had halted and was waiting by a corner bus stop seventy or eighty yards away.

Jessica considered. The problem now was going to be to get close to the girl—and actually follow her onto the bus—without being spotted. If only there were a few other waiting passengers she could hide among, but at present Ashley was the only one.

The next moment Jessica's problem was, in one sense, solved: as she stood wavering, a bus swept past her from behind. It drew up at the stop, Ashley hopped nimbly aboard, and the bus moved off.

Jessica could have wept from sheer frustration. To have come so close, and then . . .

But no! She wouldn't be beaten!

Traffic ahead of the bus was heavy. Already it was slowing down. It *must* be possible to catch it.

A taxi!

Jessica ran to the curb, searching the traffic stream for a cab. Almost immediately she spotted one. She threw up a hand and called.

It passed by, unheeding. Occupied.

Jessica cast a despairing glance toward the back of the bus. It didn't seem to have progressed much farther. But obviously this couldn't last. At any moment the traffic ahead was bound to clear.

Another occupied cab passed. Then at last one responded to Jessica's frenzied waves. She gave a sigh of relief, stepped off the curb, and spoke urgently through the window to the driver.

"Follow that bus." She pointed down the street.

She had her hand on the passenger door. But then she noticed that the driver was staring at her in disbelief.

"Are you kidding, lady?" he said. "D'you know where that thing's going?" And before she could get the door open, he pulled away into the traffic stream.

"No, I do *not!*" Jessica yelled. *"That* is the problem!"

She stood in the road, staring furiously after the taxi. Amazingly, she could still just see Ashley's bus. But obviously now the situation was hopeless.

The next second Jessica nearly leaped in the air, as from behind her came a raucous horn blast. She spun around and saw a bus bearing down on her. About to leap for the sidewalk, Jessica suddenly realized that this was her final chance.

There was no time to reflect. She took a deep breath, raised her arm in an authoritative halt signal, and stood her ground. The bus, its horn still blaring, continued to hurtle toward her. She closed her eyes and prayed.

There was a harsh squeal of brakes. Jessica stood stiff, waiting for the terrifying noise to stop. Eventually it did so and she opened her eyes. The front of the bus had come to rest about three feet from her. The driver was glaring and gesticulating at her through the windshield.

"Thank heavens," Jessica murmured devoutly.

She trotted hastily to the side of the vehicle and made to step on board. Her left foot was actually off the ground when suddenly the bus jerked forward, leaving her still standing in the road.

She stared after it speechlessly. Then, once again, she started to run.

The bus came to a halt by the stop at which Ashley had boarded, and a couple of passengers alighted. Panting, Jessica arrived in the nick of time and mounted the step just as the driver was about to close the doors. She clung to the pole, trying to get her breath, and he looked coldly at her.

"You!" he grunted. "Tired of life, lady?"

"Far from it," she answered with dignity.

She heard someone in the doorway behind her and moved to one side. Rummaging in her purse, she allowed a burly young black man to push past her. He dropped some coins in the farebox and took a seat about halfway down the aisle.

The bus moved forward. Having found a dollar bill,

Jessica looked up and peered through the windshield. The other bus was now about a block and a half away.

She addressed the driver. "Excuse me, but does this bus go to the same place as that bus up ahead?"

He sighed as though the burdens of the world were on his shoulders.

"That's the way it works, lady. Up the street, down the street. Seventy-five cents."

"Oh, good."

She held her dollar bill out to him. He ignored it.

"Exact change, lady." He pointed to a notice on the coin receptacle.

"But I don't have the exact change," Jessica said wearily.

"Then off you get at the next stop."

She bridled. "I will do no such thing."

"Yes, you will."

"You mean you'll hurl me off bodily?"

"Nope. I'll just sit here till a cop comes along and does it for me. Unless the other passengers get a bit fed up and decide to do it themselves."

In desperation, Jessica glanced once again through the windshield. Ashley's bus was still in sight—just. She looked the opposite way and let her eyes run over the other passengers. Most stared stonily ahead, apparently completely uninterested, and seemingly most unlikely to attempt a mass assault upon her person.

Only the young black man was watching her—with, she fancied, a rather odd expression. As he saw her looking at him, he glanced hastily away, out of the window.

Then her gaze fell on a very large old lady in the front seat. She was bestowing a wide, twinkly smile upon Jessica. Delighted at the sight of a friendly face, Jessica was about to smile back when she noticed something that seemed completely inexplicable. Around the old lady's considerable girth was hanging a change dispenser.

Jessica stared for a moment, then leaned toward her, holding out her bill. "Excuse me," she said politely, "but would you have four quarters for a dollar?"

Without ceasing to smile, the old lady shook her head. "No."

Jessica blinked. "I beg your pardon?"

"Said I ain't. What I do have is *three* quarters for a dollar."

Light dawned on Jessica. "I see."

Resignedly, she handed over the bill and received three quarters in return.

"Do many people get on board without the right change?" she asked.

"You'd be surprised, dearie."

"Nothing would surprise me," Jessica said. "You must do quite well out of it."

"Beats welfare, any day."

Jessica dropped the quarters in the receptacle and then looked once more through the windshield at the bus ahead. She fancied they might have gained on it slightly in the last minute. She continued standing, not taking her eyes off the vehicle in front. She had no idea where the stops were situated on this route, and at any moment the bus might halt and Ashley alight.

Suddenly the driver spoke again.

"Lady, for seventy-five cents, you're entitled to a seat."

"Oh, I'm fine like this, thank you," she said.

"Will you sit down!"

Jessica looked at him sadly and clicked her tongue. "You

know"—she bent and looked at his badge—"you know, George, rudeness does not become you."

Steam was by now practically coming out of the driver's ears. He opened his mouth, fully primed to emit some choice expletives. But Jessica, who still had her eyes fixed on the bus ahead, laid a soothing hand on his arm.

'Wait a moment," she said sharply.

He swung around and glared at her, his eyes bulging. "Whaddya mean, wait a moment? I'm driving a bus."

"That one is stopping."

"What?" He looked front again. Then he gave a snort that nearly choked him. "Of course it's stopping, you silly old bag! That's a stop! What are you trying to . . ."

But Jessica wasn't listening. Ashley had stepped off the other bus and was walking back along the sidewalk.

"Stop here, please," Jessica said suddenly.

The driver gave a groan of despair.

'George, I'd like to get off. Quickly, please. It's very important."

Abruptly, George slammed on the brakes and the bus lurched to a stop. Jessica, gripping the pole, just managed to maintain her balance.

George was staring at her with grim satisfaction.

"I'm only supposed to open the doors at official stops," he said quietly. "Except in cases of emergency. Lady, you *are* an emergency. A walking emergency. Please"—he touched a control, opening both the front and rear doors of the bus—"get off. Back or front, but just get off. Now!"

She stepped down onto the street. Then she turned. "George," she called, "it's been delightful. We must do this again."

The bus roared off. Jessica did not notice that another passenger had emerged from the rear doors at the last moment and had moved silently into the shadow of a nearby doorway, where he silently watched her. It was the young black man.

But Jessica's attention was given entirely to Ashley Vickers, whom she could still see a hundred yards away. Now Ashley was coming toward her.

How best to keep Ashley under observation was the problem. Jessica knew that if she waited at this point, there was the danger the girl would turn off down some side street and would disappear again before she herself could reach it. On the other hand, if Jessica walked toward her, and Ashley did *not* turn off, they might end up meeting face-to-face. Although such an encounter would not be the disaster here it would have been in Ashley's office, it would put an end to discovering whom the girl was going to meet. Jessica could hope to rely on finding some alleyway or niche to dart into at the last minute. But it would be a risk.

She was just telling herself that she had only moments to reach a decision when, for the second time that evening, a decision was made for her. For Ashley paused, gave a somewhat furtive glance around her, and then quickly disappeared through the door of some building that Jessica could not at this distance identify.

Jessica hurried forward, being careful not to take her eyes for one instant from the spot at which Ashley had disappeared.

As she drew closer she could see that the building in question was brightly lit. Some kind of store? A bar? No. She was now close enough to see that the place was a small café.

Jessica drew level with it. A garish little place, its stonework crumbling, its windows plastered with posters.

Keeping her head turned away, Jessica hurried past and stopped in the doorway of a TV store abutting the café. She considered. This was a most unlikely place for the elegant Ashley to have a rendezvous. No doubt there was a good reason, if only that she would be extremely unlikely to encounter any of her other friends here.

Jessica longed to know whether the person Ashley had arranged to meet was already in the café. If so, it might only be necessary to walk boldly through the door to face the murderer of Dexter Baxendale.

On the other hand, if Ashley was so far merely waiting, to go in now could ruin everything. Or it might be that Ashley and her unknown friend had retired to some back room, and that by going in Jessica would learn absolutely nothing.

It really seemed that she had no choice but to wait and see.

She looked around her and for the first time became fully conscious of her immediate surroundings.

Oh dear. This really was a pretty grim neighborhood. Litter everywhere, graffiti, loungers wandering aimlessly back and forth, ragged alcoholics lurching about, prostitutes chatting in little groups or strutting up and down. So incredibly different from Cabot Cove that it might be another world. Or at least a movie set.

But if this *were* a movie, seen on TV from the comfort and safety of her living room, with the press of a button she could switch it all off. *These* people couldn't be switched off. They were very much there, and it was clear some of them were becoming as conscious of her as she was of them.

Jessica realized that in this neighborhood she must stick out like a sore thumb: the personification of conservative, middle-class respectability—and of comparative affluence.

Jessica came to a sudden decision. She had to know whether Ashley had yet met with her phone friend, or whether she was still waiting. She couldn't wait here any longer, a cynosure for all eyes, and not do anything.

She took a deep breath and stepped out firmly from her doorway.

Perhaps it wouldn't be necessary to go inside the café; a quick peek through the window might be sufficient. And it was fairly bright inside; it might not be possible from there to see much that occurred outside.

Speed was the important thing: not to give the girl, if she was watching the street, too long to be sure of just whom she had seen.

Jessica fairly shot up to the café window, put her face against the glass, and blinked into the interior. For a few seconds she could make out nothing. Then . . . yes! There was Ashley. And she was alone. What was more, she had her back to the door. Jessica relaxed slightly and studied her for a moment.

The girl was sitting at a small table against the wall. She was smoking with quick, nervous movements of her hands. In front of her was an apparently untouched cup of muddy-looking coffee. Several of the other patrons were casting interested glances in her direction. She seemed oblivious to them, no doubt being used to this reaction wherever she went.

As Jessica watched, Ashley looked up at a big clock on the wall. It showed exactly nine p.m. She glanced at her watch, as if to confirm this, then got to her feet and opened her purse.

Jessica scurried quickly away. She gazed around in a mild

panic, spotted a deserted and darkened store with a deep entryway a few yards down the street, hurried along, and stood well back in it.

She watched the café door, and a moment later Ashley emerged and walked off briskly in the opposite direction.

Jessica thanked her lucky stars she had decided to look through the window. Had she remained in the TV store doorway, she would now almost certainly have assumed that Ashley had completed her meeting—and would have waited to see who emerged from the café after Ashley got clear. By the time she had discovered her error she would have lost the girl for good.

Jessica let Ashley get a lead, then started off after her.

This was all decidedly odd. Ashley presumably had had no rendezvous in that café after all. It surely couldn't be that she had just suddenly got tired of waiting: she couldn't have been in there more than ten or twelve minutes.

No. The way the girl had checked the time indicated a prior decision to leave there exactly on the hour. She had just been filling in time until her "talk" could take place somewhere else. Yet what an odd spot to choose to wait in.

However, speculation at this stage was useless. The important thing was not to lose her again.

Ashley was now striding briskly along. And even though many heads were turning to look at her, she seemed impervious to her surroundings and quite unaware of possible danger. She was either a remarkably brave or a remarkably foolish girl. And it seemed clear that she did not know she was being followed.

Ashley was not slackening her pace at all, and Jessica felt thankful that she kept so fit: Ashley was much younger than she was. It had been a long and tiring day, and her legs were beginning to ache. But there was no question of having to abandon the expedition. She'd collapse in the street first.

Chapter Eleven

TO Jessica's relief, Ashley's pace finally slowed. Jessica let herself draw slightly closer. The girl still did not look behind, but she had started glancing around. It seemed she might be getting a little edgy. Could the end of her journey be near?

Then, without warning, she turned abruptly at right angles and disappeared from Jessica's sight.

Jessica broke into a run and quickly reached the spot at which the girl had vanished.

She discovered that Ashley had simply turned down a narrow alley between two large, dark buildings. Jessica gazed along the alley.

It looked most forbidding. It was long and narrow and illuminated by only two dim lamps. Ashley was just passing under the first of these. At the far end could be seen the lights and traffic of the street running parallel to the one Jessica was on.

She hesitated, then squared her shoulders. Anywhere Ashley Vickers could go, Jessica Fletcher could go too.

She stepped resolutely into the alley.

She had gone about twenty-five yards when she heard the footsteps behind her.

She felt a sudden prickling up her spine. The impulse to glance back was enormous. But she resisted it and simply increased her pace. Immediately the footsteps behind her also quickened.

Jessica broke into a run. She came to the small pool of light cast by the first lamp and passed out of it into the virtual blackness beyond. The footsteps were now running too.

She told herself that if she could only reach the street at the far end, she might yet be safe.

She tried to run faster. But the ground underfoot was pot-holed and rutted. In the darkness she kept stumbling.

Gasping with exhaustion and fear, she was approaching the second of the lamps. Suddenly a big figure loomed up from the side of the alley in front of her.

Jessica ran straight into his arms. She could see almost nothing of him, but could tell he was big and obviously young.

She heard him chuckle. "Not so fast, mama."

She opened her mouth to scream, but he must have sensed rather than seen her intention, for he suddenly clasped a hand over her mouth.

She jerked her head back and bit his hand hard.

He gave a yell and momentarily his grip loosened. Jessica pushed him as hard as she could and again started to run.

As she did so, she caught a brief glimpse of Ashley at the far end of the alley, staring back. Then the girl moved quickly out of sight.

Jessica heard an urgent voice shout behind her.

"What happened?"

"She bit me!"

"You zombie! After her, quick!"

She carried on running as fast as she could, but it was hopeless. They caught up with her under the second lamp, grabbed her by the arms, and forced her back against the wall.

She got her first good look at them. They appeared oddly alike—in their late teens or early twenties, long-haired, lean and pale, and with something strange about their eyes. Junkies, she said to herself.

She continued to struggle and had the satisfaction of kicking one of them sharply on the shin.

He swore and gripped her more tightly. Then he put his face up close against hers. He hissed: "All we wanted was the purse, mama. But just for that—and the bite—we're gonna give you a free blood test."

There was an ominous click, and she saw the glint of a knife blade appear in front of her eyes.

For the second time a hand was clapped over her mouth, and this time she could not dislodge it. She watched with horrified eyes as the point of the knife was brought slowly closer and closer to her face.

Then there was an intervention.

Inexplicably, from somewhere in the darkness a hand shot out and twisted sharply at the wrist of the knifeman.

He gave a howl of pain and the blade clattered to the ground.

The next moment the space around her was a maelstrom of action. She heard punches land. Gasps. Thuds. Yelps of pain. Somebody fell heavily. A fist whizzed past, an inch from her nose. She leaned up against the wall, gasping for breath, nearly fainting.

Suddenly she heard a voice call hoarsely: "Split!"

Then she became aware of someone clambering to his feet, and of two sets of footsteps retreating down the alley.

After that, all was silence.

Jessica shook her head dazedly, looked up, and managed to get her eyes focused. Staring down at her, a concerned expression on his face, was the young black man from the bus.

"You all right, ma'am?" he asked gently.

Jessica nodded dumbly.

"They didn't hurt you?"

She was getting her breath back. She gulped. "No, I'm all right. Thank you very much."

"You're welcome."

Jessica was fast recovering her wits—also, remembering why she was here. And a realization suddenly hit her. Everything in the alley had happened fantastically quickly. It was certainly still less than a minute since she had last seen Ashley.

She grabbed the young man by the lapels.

"Please—do something else for me?"

"Sure."

"Run to the end of the alley, quick as you can. Turn right. Look for a girl. Beautiful. Black hair. Wearing a blood-red suit and white blouse. Follow her. Find out where she goes. I'll make it worth your while, I promise."

"What about you?"

"I'll be okay. I'll wait for you at the end of the alley. Only please hurry. It's desperately urgent."

He gave a quick nod, turned, and ran off at an easy lope. At the end of the alley she saw him outlined for a second against the lights of the street. Then he was gone.

Jessica slowly and painfully made her way in the same direction. Suddenly she felt very old.

She emerged from the alley into the bright lights of the street. She blinked around, saw a low window ledge, walked across, and gratefully sank down on it.

Then she closed her eyes and tried to collect herself. After a few minutes she felt better and opened her eyes again.

What absolutely appalling luck that mugging had been. Just when, she felt sure, she had been within minutes of seeing the end of Ashley's journey.

On the other hand, it wasn't bad luck but her own foolishness in venturing into such a place alone that had gotten her into trouble.

Jessica's train of thought came to a sudden halt.

That was very odd. Those youths must have planned the mugging, because one of them had been lurking in the alley in advance, while the other had come up from behind. Yet there was no way they could have known *she* was going into the alley. They surely wouldn't have expected *anyone* to venture into it alone, at night; therefore, it couldn't have been just a question of hoping a possible victim might happen along.

So they must have been waiting for Ashley. But no. That couldn't be. The one who had already been in the alley had let Ashley pass.

It didn't make sense. Unless he had spotted her, Jessica, following Ashley, and decided to let the girl go and concentrate the attack on this second person instead.

That was possible. However, if the mugging had been planned, that meant that someone—presumably the man who had called Ashley's office—had tipped them off as to her movements.

And that made it a whole new ball game.

Then again, where did the black youth come into the picture?

He must have followed her all the way from the bus. Why?

She gave a deep sigh. It was all too much. She'd been a fool to get involved like this. What had made her think, just because she had a knack for creating and solving fictional mysteries, that she was qualified to solve a real-life one? Much better to have left it to the professionals.

"Ma'am?"

Jessica looked up with a start. The young black was standing over her.

She got quickly to her feet, her heart sinking. "No luck?" she asked quietly.

He hesitated. "Well, I think maybe . . ."

Jessica caught her breath. "What do you mean?"

"I saw a girl who looked like the one you described. I followed her."

Jessica's fatigue suddenly lifted. "And what happened?" she asked eagerly.

"She went into this building. I figured she might be in there hours, so I came back for you."

"Yes, you did quite right. What building was it?"

"I'll take you there. It's not far."

"Yes, please."

They set off, Jessica practically trotting to keep up with his loping, long-legged stride.

He said: "Maybe she left after I came back for you."

"I don't think so," Jessica said decidedly.

They rounded a corner and suddenly the young man stopped. He pointed.

"That's where the lady went."

136

Jessica stood still and stared at the building he indicated. She looked behind her at the street sign and her expression changed. Then she walked slowly forward and read a notice on the door of the building.

A great feeling of triumph welled up within her. She'd done it!

The young man came up to her shoulder. "Want me to come in with you?"

She turned to him with a smile of pure contentment. "No, thank you. I'm not going in—now. I've found out all I need to know." She couldn't resist sharing her triumph. "Do you know what I've just done, er . . . ?" She paused interrogatively.

"Oh, Joe."

"Do you know what I've . . ." She corrected herself. ". . . what *we've* just done, Joe? We have just solved a murder."

His eyebrows went up. "We have? That's great. And what are you . . . we . . . goin' to do now?"

Jessica took a deep breath. "The first thing I'm going to do is have a drink. Will you join me, Joe?"

Joe found a fairly respectable bar, and ten minutes later they were sitting in a corner booth, sipping their drinks. Jessica had made a strong effort to repair the ravages the night had made on her appearance. With her immediate mission accomplished, her weight off her feet, and refreshment in front of her, she was feeling quite her old self.

Joe was regarding her thoughtfully.

"Sure like to know what this is all about," he said.

"Oh, you will, Joe, I promise. But not yet. I have a lot of thinking to do first. Now." She opened her purse. "I promised I'd make this worth your while."

"There's no need for that, ma'am."

"Well, let's argue about that later. First, I want to know what this is all about."

He shifted in his seat. "What do you mean?"

"I want to know why you tailed me tonight."

"I didn't tail . . ."

"Oh, but you did. You followed me onto the bus and you must have gotten off when I did. Then obviously you were right behind me all the way, or you could never have rescued me so quickly in that alley. Now, why?"

He shrugged. "I did follow you onto the bus. I was hoping to talk to you. But you hopped off so quick I didn't get a chance. I figured you were in some sort of trouble. Now, I know this neighborhood. Some awful bad people hang around here. Lady on her own's likely to find herself in need of a friend. So I decided to tag along and make sure you were okay."

Jessica eyed him thoughtfully. "Well, that's wonderful, Joe. I'm more grateful than I can say. But you still haven't explained why you wanted to speak to me."

"Well, Mrs. Fletcher, you're a celebrity, you know."

She stared. "You know who I am."

"Sure. Seen you on TV. Besides, I had this, with your picture on the back."

And to Jessica's astonishment, he reached into his jacket pocket and brought out a copy of *The Corpse Danced at Midnight*.

"I been reading this," he went on. "I think it's really great."

She said weakly: "And that's all you wanted to say to me?"

"Well, not completely." He pushed the book across the

table toward her. "I wanted to ask you to autograph my copy."

In the lobby of Jessica's hotel, three people were waiting. All were plainly anxious. Preston Giles fidgeted and glanced constantly at his watch. On a sofa opposite him sat Grady. He was trying to occupy himself by studying several sheets of computer printout, but he glanced up toward the doors every time somebody came in. Next to Grady sat Kitt, nervously smoking a cigarette.

"Well, Grady, I have to say it," Preston said suddenly. "I think it was rather irresponsible of you to go along with her in this scheme."

Grady sighed. "Mr. Giles, you don't know my aunt as well as I do. She was dead set on it. And when Aunt Jess is dead set on anything . . . well, *I* can't stop her."

"But chasing around New York City at night . . . alone . . . maybe following a killer."

"I explained I hadn't a clue she was doing that," Grady said. "When she wasn't in Ashley's office and I went looking for her, I was staggered when Tom told me Ashley had been there and Aunt Jess had gone racing after her. And all to return a pen, according to him."

"Well," Kitt said, "we realize that was a blind, of course."

Preston gave a groan. "But what happens if Ashley discovers she's being followed?"

"Well, naturally, I'm anxious too," Kitt said, "but not so much as you two. I think Aunt Jess . . . Mrs. Fletcher . . . can take care of herself." She stubbed out her cigarette, looked up, and then jumped to her feet. "And I'm right!"

Preston and Grady followed her gaze and hastily rose as

they saw Jessica entering the hotel. She started to make for the desk, then saw them and changed direction.

Preston gave an exclamation. "Jessica! Thank heavens!"

"Aunt Jess, where on earth have you been?" Grady said urgently. "We've been worried stiff."

"Well, you needn't worry anymore. As you can see, I'm perfectly all right."

She sat down and smiled around at them.

"What have you been doing?" Kitt asked.

"Solving the murder."

They stared at her. "You mean you know who killed Baxendale?" Grady said incredulously.

"I know who was behind the murder, if not who pulled the trigger."

"But who?" They all spoke together.

Jessica considered. Then she shook her head. "I'm not saying yet."

"Really, Jessica!" For the first time since she'd known him, Preston sounded quite irritated with her.

"Now, Preston, you must allow me my sense of drama and suspense. I *am* a mystery writer, after all."

Her eyes fell on the computer printouts in Grady's hands. "Oh, are those the real estate sales figures I asked you for, dear?"

He looked awkward. "Actually, no. I must have hit the wrong button. These seem to be last year's wholesale fish prices." He paused, then added defensively: "Well, I was nervous."

"I'm sure they make riveting reading," Jessica said. "Thankfully, we shan't need those other figures, after all."

"We won't?"

"No."

"But why?"

"Wouldn't you like to know."

Grady became exasperated. "Aunt Jess, you told me once that you hate those mystery stories in which people keep vital information to themselves for absolutely no reason. And now you're doing that very same thing."

"And you know what invariably happens?" Preston put in grimly. "Those people always get knocked off before they can tell what they know."

"Now, don't get fiction confused with real life, you two. Besides, I have no intention of keeping vital information to myself for long. First, however, I want something to eat. You did promise me dinner tonight, you know, Preston. I realize I'm a *little* late, but how about us all going out for something? Then I promise I'll tell all."

Jessica drank the last few drops of coffee in her cup and wiped her mouth with a napkin.

"That was a delightful meal, Preston. Thank you."

The four of them were in a small, quiet, and very expensive restaurant near Coventry House. It was a place Preston frequently patronized when he had business to discuss, because there was ample space between the tables and it was possible to speak perfectly freely without being overheard.

"Glad you liked it," he said. "Now, Jessica, please . . ."

"Very well." She paused to collect her thoughts. "You know Ashley Vickers came to her office while I was searching it. I had a minute's warning and hid in the bathroom. She took some papers from a locked drawer. Then the phone rang. She had a very interesting conversation, the strong implication of which was that she *is* the one who's been leaking information. But more important, she actually said, 'I told you that after this is over I won't have any part in murder.' "

"Good Lord!" Preston said.

Grady gave a whistle. "But that's fantastic!"

"Not all that fantastic. You see, there were no other witnesses, so there's no corroboration."

"But who was she talking to?" Kitt asked.

"That's what I didn't know. But then the person on the other end obviously asked her to come and see him—right away. She agreed, which is why, clearly, I had to follow her. Even though it meant walking out on you, Grady."

He nodded. "I can see that. Though I wish you hadn't taken the risk. It was terrifically brave of you."

"Oh, fiddle-faddle. Anyway, I followed her quite a long way, first on a bus and then on foot. I had one or two little adventures en route, and nearly lost her . . ."

"What sort of adventures?" Preston asked sharply.

"I'll tell you all about it some other time. The important thing is that I did discover where Ashley went." She paused.

"And saw who she met?" Kitt asked eagerly.

"Not exactly *saw.*"

Grady's face fell. "Then I can't understand . . ."

"Patience, Grady. You see, it was the building she entered that gave it away."

"Well, what building was it?" Preston asked.

"A theatre. The Serendipity Theatre, to be exact."

They all looked blank. Preston said: "I've never heard of it."

"I'm not surprised. It's very small and shabby, one of those hole-in-the-wall storefront theatres tucked away in a commercial area. Its precise location is just off Seventeenth Street."

Still they all stared at her without reaction.

Jessica said: "Perhaps none of you were there when it was mentioned, but as soon as I saw Seventeenth Street on the sign, I remembered."

"Remembered what, for Pete's sake?" Grady demanded.

"Something that was said at the party. I hardly had to go up and look at the poster on the door."

"Poster?" Preston queried.

"Yes. It said that they were holding tryouts for a new musical by Peter Brill."

Preston's face was a study. "Peter? *He's* the killer? I can't believe it. He just doesn't seem the type."

"I don't know," Kitt said. "He's pretty bitter. Seems to dislike everything and everybody."

"So did Jonathan Swift," Preston exclaimed. "So did Ambrose Bierce. They didn't kill people. Besides, with Peter I'm sure the bitterness is just a reaction against the bad luck he's been having. He simply seems too fastidious to blow a man's face away with a shotgun." Kitt winced. Grady coughed.

Jessica broke the silence. "Peter Brill may not have done the shooting himself. Perhaps he paid somebody else to pull the trigger."

Preston shook his head. "I can't even see him doing that."

"I admire your loyalty to a friend, Preston, but it's

amazing what people will do when they're desperate for money.''

"You think he's desperate?'' Grady said.

"I believe so, yes. His lack of success recently is hurting him deeply. Preston, you yourself said that he's been scared his talent is gone for good. This musical could be his last chance. I remember hearing him say it takes a quarter of a million just to get started—money which apparently he's found, or believes he can get. Now, Mr. McCallum told me today that that report could have been worth big, big money to somebody if it fell into the wrong hands. It would have been a godsend to Brill, even after Ashley had taken her cut. Remember, too, there have been other costly leaks from McCallum Enterprises before, which is why Dexter Baxendale was called in.''

"Then what exactly do you figure happened Saturday night, Aunt Jess?'' Grady asked.

"Well, Ashley took the report down to hand over to Brill at the party. It was a risk, but they were playing for very high stakes. Brill no doubt had the contacts enabling him to dispose of the report in the most profitable quarter. Now, she arrived at your place with the Captain before Brill, didn't she?'' She raised her eyebrows at Preston.

He nodded. Jessica went on: "So she couldn't dispose of it immediately. Even after Brill arrived, however, she must have realized that there was a possibility she was under surveillance and had to be very cautious about handing it over. And while she was waiting, Baxendale found the report. We don't know what he was doing in your room, Grady, but I think it quite possible Ashley hid the report there and that's where Baxendale found it.''

Grady stared. "You mean she was intending to frame me?"

"Not strictly. Obviously, she hoped it wouldn't be found at all. But if it *was*, she'd clearly rather it be found in your room. The vital point is that Baxendale got hold of the report. Ashley discovered this—no doubt guessed the worst as soon as she heard about the intruder—and immediately reported to Brill."

Jessica broke off, took a sip of water, then continued. "Brill must have been frantic at the thought of losing all that money, so he went after Baxendale. As a result, Baxendale was shot, either by Brill or by a thug working for him. But from Brill's viewpoint it was too late. Baxendale had already taken the report to his car, locked it in, and had come back—hoping, I believe, for a cut in the profit or to apply a spot of blackmail. So although his death did save Brill from exposure, it didn't get him the report back."

There was silence for a few moments while they all digested what had been said.

Grady was the first to speak. "It all fits in. No snags that I can see."

"I wouldn't go quite as far as that, dear," Jessica said. "There are a few snags, but none that can't be surmounted."

She frowned and looked suddenly thoughtful.

"What's the matter?" he said.

"I'm just wondering if one can surmount a snag." She gave a firm nod. "Yes, one can—quite correct usage."

He gave a groan. "English teachers! Authors!"

"What do you think those papers were that Ashley took from her desk?" Kitt asked suddenly.

"Probably a duplicate of the report. Brill must have asked her for it today, so she went along to the office tonight to get the photocopy while no one was around. Meanwhile, Brill found he could dispose of it—and get paid for it—tonight. So he took the chance of calling Ashley's office and caught her while she was there. He told her to bring the papers straight to him at the Serendipity Theatre, and she did so."

"Good Lord!" Grady suddenly looked alarmed. "That means the report's probably already in the wrong hands. I ought to warn McCallum quick."

Jessica raised her eyebrows. "In spite of the way he's treated you?"

He looked awkward. "Well, I owe the firm some sort of loyalty."

She patted his hand. "Good boy. But actually you needn't worry. The Captain told me today that that report would only be valuable to outsiders if he acted on its recommendation. He only let it be *thought* he was going to."

Grady relaxed. "Oh, I see."

Kitt gave a frown. "Wouldn't Ashley know that?"

"I don't think so," Jessica said. "There's certainly no intimacy between her and the captain now. And I don't suppose she was at work today, was she, Grady?"

He shook his head. "I don't believe so."

"She wasn't," Preston said. "I called in to see Caleb late this afternoon. He'd just arrived there from his yacht. He happened to mention she hadn't been in."

"There you are. As far as she's concerned, the position regarding the report is the same as it was before the weekend."

Grady grinned. "Poor old Brill's really going to be in hot

water if he sells the report for a fat profit, and then the buyers find out it's worthless.''

"Well," Kitt said, "what's the next move, Aunt Jess? I mean, Mrs. Fletcher . . ." She stopped. "Sorry."

"Please do call me Aunt Jess, Kitt. I think it's a very good sign."

"Thank you," Kitt said. "I was going to say, hadn't you better tell the police what you've found out?"

"No, I don't think so."

"Oh, but surely . . ."

"What do you think, Preston?" Jessica asked.

Somewhat reluctantly, he shook his head. "No, I agree with you, Jessica."

He looked at Kitt. "Jessica realizes that we have absolutely nothing the police could act on. It's pure suspicion—logically based, I agree, but completely without substantiation."

"But Ashley's going to see Peter tonight . . ."

"That's no crime," Jessica said. "Why shouldn't she go and watch a friend holding auditions for a new show?"

Grady grew insistent. "But, Aunt Jess, Chief Gunderson respects your opinion. You told me he more or less asked you to put your mind to the problem. If you told him your deductions, it would at least make him think."

"Perhaps," she said. "But since he spoke to me in the car, he's become very suspicious of you. I fear he'd think my theory was cunningly contrived to get you off the hook. Besides, it seems the county detectives have taken over the case from him. Matter of jurisdiction, he said. And I don't think *they'd* take too kindly to my butting in."

Kitt banged the table in frustration. "But there must be something we can do!"

Jessica nodded thoughtfully. "I think that probably our best bet is a frontal attack on Peter Brill himself."

"How do you mean?" Grady asked.

"Well, on the phone Ashley told him not to get hysterical. With a murder and robbery hanging over him, and at the same time trying to put on a new show, he must be living very much on his nerves. If he was suddenly confronted with the information that I know of his involvement, he might well panic. And he might be pushed into making a serious blunder."

"Yes—such as trying to kill you," Grady said grimly.

"Well, that would be excellent," Jessica said. "The best thing that could possibly happen, especially if there were witnesses."

"Now, Jessica, don't be foolhardy," Preston cautioned. "You've taken quite enough risks today already."

She looked at him quizzically. "Where is the risk, Preston, if, as you say, Peter Brill is not the type to commit murder?"

He spread his hands. "You've got me there. I still feel that about him. But if there's the slightest chance of danger, I don't want you risking it."

"I don't really believe for a moment he'll try to harm me. And I promise I won't take any risks, Preston."

"Then I suppose I must give my blessing—partly to preserve my self-respect, because it won't make a blind bit of difference if I don't." He smiled at the truth of his statement.

"When will you talk to Brill?" Kitt asked.

"Tomorrow, I think. At the theatre. Judging by the poster, he should be there most of the day You can drive me, if you will, Grady."

"Yes, sure."

She pushed her chair back and got to her feet. "And now it's me for my hotel—and bed. This has really been quite a day."

Chapter Twelve

AT ten o'clock the next morning Grady's sports car pulled up at the curb outside the Serendipity Theatre. Grady got out, went around to the sidewalk, and opened the passenger door. Jessica, with his assistance and some difficulty, extracted herself.

Grady opened the theatre door. From within they immediately heard the distant tinkle of a piano.

"Sounds of life," Grady remarked. "Look, Aunt Jess, I'm still not happy about letting you go in there and confront him alone."

"Grady, he wouldn't dare try to harm me here. Not when I make it clear that other people know I've come to see him. You stay just where you are. Keep an eye on that lovely car—and an ear open for me. If he attacks me, I'll scream. I assure you, Fay Wray has nothing on me when I'm in full voice. Then will be the time for the fighting CPA to go into action."

She gave him a wink and disappeared into the theatre.

Jessica crossed a small foyer, pushed open another door, and emerged into an auditorium. It was in darkness, but the light from a bare, uncurtained stage revealed this as a small, cramped theatre with a general air of tattiness. It smelled both stuffy and musty.

On the stage were three people. At center was a young lady of obvious physical endowments, but considerably less musical talent, struggling to perform a song with little tune and an unrhyming lyric. Nearby a flashily dressed man was seated backward astride an old kitchen chair, gazing at the singer with an expression of intense delight. Seated at an upright piano downstage and providing accompaniment was Peter Brill. On his face was a look of anguish that nicely counterbalanced the other man's expression, reminding Jessica of the before and after sections of an indigestion-tablet advertisement.

She made her way quietly about halfway to the front, lowered herself onto an extremely uncomfortable aisle seat, and settled down to listen.

For one raised on the musicals of Kern, Rodgers, Gershwin, and Berlin it was a painful experience. If this was a typical number, could Brill's new show ever make the grade? She knew tastes had changed, but had they really changed this much?

After a few more minutes the routine blessedly came to an end. The flashy-looking man applauded enthusiastically and got to his feet, beaming. "Well, Petey boy, ain't she great?"

Brill rubbed his eyes. "Marvin," he said wearily, "your client's talent is exceeded only by her monumental capacity for flagellation of the treble clef."

"You got it," the agent said happily.

The singer put her hands on her hips and stared at Brill. "We through?" she asked peevishly. "I gotta be on the switchboard by eleven."

"I've heard all I need to, Miss Devine," Brill told her.

She sniffed. "That means I stink, right? Well, listen, buddy, you don't play so hot, either."

"But I've only had two hours' sleep," Brill said, "whereas with you, sweet thing, the oblivion of Morpheus seems to be a perpetual state of mind."

"Oh, yeah?" She clearly regarded this as a brilliant riposte.

Marvin took her by the arm. "Come on, honey, let's get out of here. Petey, I'll be in touch."

They started toward the wings, but the agent turned back and cast a quizzical eye at Brill.

"Listen, you got the dough for this thing, right?"

Brill gave him a smug smile. "Yes, Marvin, I got the dough."

Marvin shrugged and he and the girl left the stage.

Brill remained at the piano. The smug smile disappeared. Suddenly he seemed like a frightened, harried man. He played a couple of chords, then abruptly slammed the piano lid in apparent frustration.

Jessica got to her feet. She spoke loudly. "And just where did you get the dough, Mr. Brill?"

Brill gave a start and stared into the darkness. He shaded his eyes. "Who's out there? If you're here to audition, honey, come on up."

Jessica walked down the remainder of the aisle, till she was at the edge of the stage and inside the bright pool cast by the stage lighting.

Brill stared down at her in amazement. "Mrs. Fletcher! Good grief! Surely you've not come to audition?"

"Actually, I was hoping we might have a little chat."

His eyebrows went up. "Chat? About what?"

"The murder of Dexter Baxendale."

"Really? Nothing would delight me more than to hear

152

your no doubt highly ingenious theories, Mrs. Fletcher, but another time, perhaps? As you can see, I'm conducting auditions this morning and I'm expecting another performer at any moment.''

''Ah, but there's nobody here yet, so you do have a few minutes to spare, at least. My friends know I'm here, but they're not expecting me back for a while.''

''I don't really see that there's anything I can say about the murder, Mrs. Fletcher, so the exercise seems pointless.''

''Very well, then. Let's discuss your show instead.''

''That's something I'm always pleased to do. But even that will have to be brief.''

''Well, it wouldn't take long to answer the question I asked just now.''

''What was that?''

''Where you raised the dough to finance it.''

He frowned. ''I think that is my business, don't you?''

''Not solely. I take it, then, that you decline to discuss it?''

Brill got suddenly to his feet. ''Mrs. Fletcher, I've explained to you that I have a very busy day ahead.''

''So you'd like me to leave, is that it?''

''Yes, that is it.''

''I see. You won't even discuss the theft of secret documents from Caleb McCallum?''

Did she spot a momentary gleam of concern on his face? If so, it was gone quickly. ''Quite correct, Mrs. Fletcher. The matter is one of complete indifference to me.''

''I see.'' She shrugged. ''So you wouldn't be interested in the startling information I heard yesterday from the captain himself?''

She began to turn away.

"Startling?" There was a new note in Brill's voice now.

"Yes, but I won't bore you with it."

With what seemed to be a great effort, Brill smiled. "Well, now, don't let my manner upset you, Mrs. Fletcher. I do have a lot on my mind, but as an inveterate gossip, I like to be up-to-date. What is this startling information?"

"May I come onstage?"

"Please do."

Jessica mounted the few steps to the stage. Brill gave her his hand to assist her up.

"Now, where was I?" she said. "Ah, yes. Well, you know that stolen confidential report there was all that fuss about. It was found in Baxendale's car."

"I heard something about it."

"It was supposedly very valuable. But the Captain himself told me that it's quite worthless."

Brill stood perfectly still. His face did not change. If not a picture of guilt, his reaction was neither that of a man to whom the matter was one of complete indifference.

"Worthless?" he said. His voice suddenly went higher in pitch. "What do you mean?"

"Just what I say. The value of that document depended on the Captain's acting on its recommendations. He doesn't intend to do so."

Brill continued to stand quite motionless. Was it her imagination, the effects of the stage lighting, or had he gone decidedly pale?

"Surely you must be wrong?"

"Definitely not, Mr. Brill. It's quite a blow to you, isn't it? Have you actually sold the photocopy and been paid for it yet? Was that what you were up all night arranging—why you had only two hours' sleep?"

At first, it was as if he didn't take in what she was saying, but suddenly he swung around on her.

"What do you mean?" he shouted.

"You know what I mean, Mr. Brill. Ashley Vickers stole that report from the office and passed it on to you—as she has done with other information in the past."

"What utter garbage!"

"But the private detective found it," Jessice went on imperturbably, "so last night she fetched a spare photocopy from her office and brought it to you here."

"She did no such thing!"

"I followed her, Mr. Brill."

He drew his breath in sharply. *"You?* It was . . ." He broke off.

"Yes, and I have an independent witness who saw her come into this theatre."

Brill had been making a great effort to control his emotions. Now he gave a casual shrug.

"So what? Sure Ashley was here. She's taking an interest in this show and wanted to watch some of the auditions."

"And what about the papers she had locked in her office drawer and which, at your request, she brought along with her last night?"

"How did you know about that?"

The female voice rang out sharply from the wings. Jessica turned toward it.

Ashley emerged from the darkness and glared at Jessica. "I want to know how you knew about those papers."

"Oh, it's quite simple, Miss Vickers. I was in your private bathroom when you entered the office. I saw you take them."

Ashley gave a gasp. "Why, you nosy, meddling old . . ."

Jessica nodded calmly. "Yes, I am nosy, and I'm meddling. Because my nephew Grady's whole future is at stake. Which is why I'm not at all ashamed at spying on you. I consider it fully justified."

Ashley shook her head incredulously. "I don't believe this! Well, Mrs. Clever-Detective Fletcher, I'm glad your conscience is clear, because so is mine. Those papers in my desk were simply confidential reports on people in the company in line for promotion. Caleb asked me to look them over and make recommendations. I merely wanted to leave them home to study at my leisure."

"I see," Jessica said slowly, regarding her judicially. "That's not too bad a story. But I think you should fabricate something sturdier before the case comes to trial."

"What are you talking about?" Ashley said harshly. "No one can prove I stole that report."

"I think they can," Jessica said. "Now that I and my friends know of the connection between you two, I'm sure we can convince the police to dig into it. Somewhere you have quite a lot of money hidden away, Miss Vickers, which will be traced to you eventually. If you continue to deny all involvement, you will almost certainly find yourself charged as an accessory to the murder of Dexter Baxendale."

Ashley went white. But before she could speak, Brill cut in. "Accessory? Are you suggesting she was *my* accessory, Mrs. Fletcher? If so, I must inform you that at the time of that detective's unfortunate demise, I was seated at the piano, delighting my fellow guests with a few dozen melodic gems from my incomparable repertoire."

"Yes, I thought perhaps you might have a convenient alibi," Jessica said.

"Well, then?"

"To be guilty of murder, one doesn't actually have to do the deed oneself. The person who pays a hired thug to commit a killing is just as guilty as the thug himself. It would have been extremely simple for you to have smuggled someone into Preston's fancy dress party and given him detailed instructions for the disposal of Baxter."

"I am not in the habit of employing hired thugs, Mrs. Fletcher."

Jessica stared hard at him. "Aren't you, Mr. Brill?" She looked at Ashley. "Nor you, Miss Vickers?"

Seeing Ashley's discomfiture, Jessica continued her line of attack. "Last night when Mr. Brill phoned your office, he asked you to come here. You said you'd be here as soon as possible. But why did you stop off at a very cheap and nasty little café, order coffee, which you didn't drink, and stay there about ten minutes? You made a point of leaving there at exactly nine p.m. I'm certain the proprietor will remember you. You attracted quite a lot of attention."

For the second time Ashley seemed at a loss for words. She cast a despairing glance at Brill. But he avoided her eyes. Jessica thought she detected beads of perspiration on his brow.

"Would you like me to give you *my* explanation for your actions?" Jessica said.

With an attempt at casualness, Ashley shrugged. "Go ahead. I'm sure it will prove very entertaining."

"I hope it will. Well, on the phone, after agreeing to come here, you used these words: 'They may be following me.' Then you listened for quite a time while Mr. Brill plainly gave you some instructions. Eventually, you agreed to comply. Now, I don't know exactly who you thought might be following you. Perhaps the police. Perhaps operatives of Dexter Baxendale, whom Captain

McCallum had retained to shadow all the suspects. Or perhaps representatives of some rival third party after the real estate report. However, their precise identity is not relevant. Suffice it to say you were frightened of *someone's* following you here.''

She paused. Ashley, however, still did not speak. She just licked her lips.

Jessica went on. "Mr. Brill's instructions were for you to come part of the way here and then wait in that café until exactly nine o'clock. After that you were to continue on foot, being sure to pass through a certain dark alley.''

Jessica transferred her gaze to Brill. "The delay gave you time to contact a couple of young louts, whom no doubt you've had dealings with before. You gave them strict orders. Miss Vickers was to go unharmed through that alley. But the person tailing her was to be stopped, allowing Miss Vickers to proceed unmolested and unseen to this theatre. And that, Mr. Brill, is why I take with a very large pinch of salt your claim that you are not in the habit of employing hired thugs.''

Again Jessica paused. She looked from one of them to the other. For a moment Ashley seemed about to speak. But then she caught Brill's eye and obviously changed her mind.

Eventually Jessica resumed. "What you didn't know, Mr. Brill, was that there was yet another person involved, an independent witness who saw the whole thing. He followed me to the café, watched me following Miss Vickers, *and* spotted somebody shadowing me.''

Jessica gave a smile. "It really was quite a little procession. Anyway, I'm sure you know what happened. My young guardian angel took care of your thugs. It must have been quite a surprise when those young men later reported back to you that the person following Miss Vickers had been what they no doubt described as an old dame. I'm sure you spent some time puzzling out who it could have been. Which, by the way, explains your exclamation, *'You!'* when I first mentioned having followed Miss Vickers here. You nearly said, 'It was *you* they stopped.' "

At last Brill found his voice. "That's a highly ingenious scenario. Of course, you have not one iota of proof."

"There I must disagree. First there's my independent witness. He's perfectly willing to testify to everything he saw. Given that the police believe our combined account, which they're bound to, the theory I have advanced is the only logical explanation of Miss Vickers' passing through that alley unmolested. Or, in fact, for her ever walking that route. After all, if her visit here was quite innocent, her obvious course would have been to take a cab the whole way."

"It may be logical," Brill said, "but courts want hard evidence."

"They shall have that as well," Jessica said quietly. "The evidence of those two young men."

Brill went white. "What do you mean? You don't know who they were."

"Not yet. But I had a very close look at them. They're certain to have criminal records. I'll go to the police and look through the mug shots. I'll pick out those boys. They'll be arrested. And they'll talk—when I promise not to press charges if they tell who hired them."

Brill's hands were clenched at his sides. There was now no doubt about the sweat on his face. Ashley didn't look any better, and Jessica suddenly realized how fear could obliterate beauty from a face.

"All right," the girl said suddenly, "you win, Mrs. Fletcher."

Jessica and Brill both swung to face her.

Jessica caught her breath. "You mean . . . ?"

"I stole that report. I gave a photocopy of it to Peter last night."

Brill yelled at her. "Quiet, you little fool!"

At that, Ashley lost her temper. "You call *me* a fool?" she stormed. "You're too stupid to see that it's all over. She knows. Everything. It's all going to come out. All thanks to you. Doing everything on the cheap. Hiring those pathetic little creeps to do your dirty work for you. But I suppose they go along with this crummy dive and fifth-rate singers and all the rest of your shoddy little life. Why did I ever get mixed up with you? Well, this is the end. Mrs. Fletcher: I repeat, I know nothing about the murder. I'm a thief. But only a thief. I'm not taking the rap for anything else this idiot's got himself involved with. I . . ."

"Will you shut up?" Brill shouted. Then he turned on Jessica. "She's mad! Do you understand? She's flipped her lid. You repeat one word of what she said . . ."

Jessica interrupted. "I shan't repeat it. I shan't need to."

She pulled open the coat of the suit she was wearing to reveal the small tape recorder fastened to the lining. "This will do all the talking that's necessary," she said.

Brill's face went purple. "Why, you slimy old . . ."

He made a lunge toward her.

Jessica screamed.

The sheer volume of the sound in the little building took Brill aback and checked him momentarily. Jessica hastily glanced around, picked up the chair recently vacated by the agent, and held it out in front of her like a lion tamer.

"Keep back," she warned sharply.

But Brill was already advancing again. "You old bat, if you think I'm letting you walk out of here with that tape . . ."

Jessica screamed once more. The door at the back of the auditorium burst open and Grady's voice rang out.

"Hang on, Aunt Jess! I'm coming." He charged down the aisle.

Brill froze, and then seemed to deflate. He took a step back, stared at Jessica in silence for a few moments. Then, his shoulders drooping, he walked slowly away, sank down onto the piano stool, and buried his head in his hands.

Jessica lowered the chair as Grady came running up onstage and crossed to her.

"Aunt Jess, you all right?"

She gave him a rather shaky smile. "Yes, dear. I'm fine."

"What's happened?"

"Quite a lot has happened. But only one really important thing. And that, my boy, is that you have been finally and completely cleared."

Chapter Thirteen

"**T**HANK you, Sergeant. That's wonderful news. Tell Chief Gunderson we appreciate his having you let us know."

Preston Giles put down the phone and turned around.

"Ashley and Brill have signed statements admitting their involvement in the theft of the documents. Gunderson's gone to the yacht club to report to Caleb. It's official: Grady's off the hook."

Jessica gave a deep sigh. "What a relief!"

"The cops could hardly do anything else after they heard that tape, Aunt Jess." Grady gave her a kiss on the cheek. "I don't know how to thank you."

She handed him her glass. "Just fill this up again, dear."

They were in Jessica's hotel room. After taking her precious tape to the police, she and Grady had returned there for a celebration drink. Shortly after, Preston arrived to be regaled with a detailed account of the incident in the theatre.

Grady poured another drink and handed Jessica her glass.

"I suppose Brill hasn't admitted any involvement in the murder yet, Mr. Giles?"

Preston shook his head. "Vehement denials from both of them on that score. Nor is Ashley admitting anything about framing you. The sergeant said they accept she wasn't involved in the killing. But they're confident they'll make a case against Brill."

Jessica raised her eyebrows in surprise. "Well, that's more than I am."

Preston looked at her quizzically. "You think he'll have covered his tracks that well, eh?"

"Not that," she said. "I just don't think Peter Brill had anything to do with the murder of Dexter Baxendale."

Preston and Grady stared at Jessica speechlessly.

Preston was the first to find his voice. "You're not serious?"

"Oh, perfectly."

"But, Aunt Jess, you went to the theatre to try and prove he was involved."

"Not at all."

She put down her glass. "My principal concern in this case was not who killed Baxendale. As I've repeatedly said, I am not a detective and solving the murder wasn't my job. Naturally, like everybody else, I was curious. But I got involved for one reason only: to obtain proof that Ashley Vickers was responsible for the theft of that report. Because that would automatically clear you of suspicion, Grady; if you didn't steal it, you had no motive for murdering Baxendale."

"But I heard that tape," Grady said. "You virtually accused Brill of arranging the murder."

Jessica smiled. "I was a bit sneaky, I'm afraid. I was willing to say anything that might draw from either of them

163

an admission about the stolen report. I thought at one time Brill might be the killer. But it was always in the cards he would have an alibi. So in order to get him—and Ashley— rattled, I had to make up a plausible case for his having employed a hired killer. The fact that he *had* hired those two punks to stop me gave the theory feasibility. I tested it on you last night, and you seemed to think it made sense. So I then tried it out on Brill. Well, the ruse worked. Actually, of course, it was Ashley who got scared. But it didn't matter who. Once she cracked, my job was over.''

"But why don't you think Brill hired a killer?'' Preston asked. "It would, as you said, have been easy to hide somebody among all those guests in fancy dress.''

"But there's a fatal flaw in that theory. Brill didn't think of it at the time. But if he hasn't yet, his attorney soon will.''

"Well, what is it?'' Grady asked.

"It's very obvious. For Brill to have smuggled a killer into the party, he would have had to know beforehand that Baxendale was going to be there, was going to find the report, and was going to be a threat to his security. There was no way he could have known that. Nor, incidentally, is there the slightest evidence that Baxendale ever knew Brill was involved in the theft. It seems that, at the time Baxendale was shot, Brill had never even handled the document.''

Grady was thoughtful for a moment. "But suppose the target was really McCallum, as you once suggested?''

"Well, the Captain himself rather put to bed that idea when I saw him on his yacht. But the same argument would apply. Brill would never have been so foolish as to plan to have *anybody* killed under those circumstances. If he'd thought there was any danger of being exposed as a thief that night, I'm certain he would simply have arranged with Ashley to postpone the hand-over until a safer time. She wouldn't have liked it, but there would have been nothing she could have done.''

"Well, then, who do you think *did* kill Baxendale?''

"I haven't the foggiest idea. And I don't really care.''

"Oh, Aunt Jess!''

"No, Grady. Murder's a very pleasant thing to pass a few hours with—if it's in a book or on a TV screen. But real-life murder isn't at all nice. And neither, I'm afraid, are any of those people. Don't think I've enjoyed being mixed up in it.''

"What about all those deductions you were making that first morning?''

Jessica had the grace to look a little awkward. "I admit that for a short time I did get involved in the intellectual puzzle side of it. But my interest has worn very thin now. Besides, it would be virtually impossible to solve the case by deductive reasoning. We've now discovered the murder had nothing to do with the stolen documents. There were dozens of people we know of at the party, in addition to possible gate-crashers. Any one of them might have had a motive for killing Baxendale. And to check out every one of those is the sort of job only the police can tackle.''

"And you're not going to take any more interest in the case?''

"I didn't say that. I shall follow it in the papers.''

"The New York papers?'' Preston asked quietly.

Jessica looked at him enigmatically.

"If that's a way of asking if I'm staying in New York any longer, the answer is no. As you know, I've been wanting to go home for some time, but things have kept stopping me.

Now, however, there's nothing to keep me here any longer.''

''I'm sorry you should think that,'' Preston said quietly.

She smiled. ''Cabot Cove, Maine, isn't the other end of the world, Preston. I owe you a return weekend. I'd be thrilled for a chance to show off my rich and sophisticated New York publisher to all my friends.''

He grinned. ''I may take you up on that sooner than you imagine.''

''Any time. Just don't expect a fancy dress party.''

He raised his hands in mock horror. ''Please! Don't ever let me hear that phrase again.''

He got to his feet. ''I must get back to the office. I'm sure my in-tray is piled three feet high with stuff. When are you leaving?''

''Tomorrow morning, I think.''

''Dinner tonight?''

''That would be lovely.''

''Great.''

''I'd better get along to McCallum's,'' Grady said. ''I look forward to seeing the red faces when I show up again—reputation white as the driven snow.''

''Do you think the Captain's face will be red?'' Jessica asked.

''Not his. Doubt if he'll even apologize. But I'm sure going to see he asks me to stay on after all.''

''And what will you say then?''

''I shall take great pleasure in telling him to . . .'' He broke off with a grin. ''All right, Aunt Jess. I won't say it—here. Let's say I shall inform him forcefully that from now on he's going to have to manage without my invaluable services.''

"I think you're very wise, dear."

At the door Preston turned back to the young man. "Come and see me in a day or two, Grady. Publishers are always looking for good accountants, and I have lots of contacts."

Grady's face lit up. "Gee, thanks, Mr. Giles. Books would sure make a nice change from clam chowder."

Chapter Fourteen

CHIEF Roy Gunderson walked heavily along the wharf at the Bayside Yacht Club and stopped alongside the gleaming hull of the *Chowder King*.

The boat appeared deserted. He called out. "Mr. McCallum!"

He waited a few moments but nobody appeared on deck. He swore under his breath. They'd told him at McCallum's office that the Captain was spending the day on his yacht. But it looked to Gunderson as if he might have had a wasted journey. It would, of course, have been easy to phone McCallum, or send a subordinate. But Gunderson, on whom the Captain's insult of Sunday morning still grated, had been looking forward to seeing McCallum's face when he was told that Ashley had been the traitor all along. It seemed, though, that this was a pleasure he was going to have to forgo.

Gunderson started to turn away. Then he hesitated. McCallum might be sleeping. Besides, he might not be alone.

Gunderson grinned to himself. If so, there could be a laugh in walking in on him. It was worth a try.

He mounted the gangplank, stood for a moment looking around for signs of life, then made his way below deck. He paused outside the door of the main cabin and raised his hand to tap on the panel. Then he changed his mind, took hold of the knob, turned it, and walked straight in.

To his disappointment, the cabin was deserted. He was about to go out again when his eye caught a dark stain on the luxurious cream carpet.

He crossed to it, stood staring at it for a couple of seconds, then knelt down and touched the stain with one finger.

Blood. Definitely blood.

Gunderson remained on his knees for half a minute, looking thoughtful. Along one wall of the cabin was a large closet, and there seemed to be another smaller stain on the floor in front of it.

He straightened up, walked across, and opened the closet door. It was full of clothes.

It was at that moment that he heard the unmistakable click of a revolver being cocked.

A voice spoke, hard and unemotional.

"Hold it, mister. Right there."

Gunderson froze. He felt, rather than heard, footsteps approaching. The voice spoke again. "Keep your hands where I can see them. Turn around—slowly."

Gunderson did so, then let his breath out. The man standing a few feet away, a .38 revolver leveled at him, was a uniformed policeman. In the doorway behind him, his revolver also drawn, was his partner.

Gunderson started to move. "Boys, for a moment you had me scared there . . ."

"*I said hold it,*" the policeman barked out. "Stand facing the wall. Hands over your head."

Gunderson complied. "I know the drill, son. My name is Roy Gunderson. I'm the chief of police up at New Holvang. My identification's in my right jacket pocket."

The two policemen exchanged glances. Then, while the one in the doorway kept his revolver trained on the chief, the first reached gingerly into Gunderson's pocket and extracted his wallet. He opened it, scanned it, then visibly relaxed.

"Sorry, Chief," he said. "Can't be too careful."

He handed Gunderson his wallet back and both policemen holstered their guns.

Gunderson returned his wallet to his pocket and eyed them curiously.

"What you boys doing here?"

"We got an anonymous tip. Said there'd been a murder on this boat."

"Did you now? Well, that may interest you, then." He pointed to the stain on the carpet.

"Blood?"

"Yeah."

"What d'you think it means, Chief?"

"Could mean he cut his hand opening a can of chowder. But in view of your tip-off, we'll take a look around. Let's go topside."

On deck again they separated and started poking around.

Then the second policeman called out. "Over here, Chief."

Gunderson joined him. The officer pointed down at the deck. What appeared to be a trail of small blood spots led toward the mainmast.

Gunderson walked slowly over to it. The mainsail was rolled and lashed. He surveyed it for a few seconds.

"You boys know anything about sailing?" he asked.

"A little, Chief," the first one said.

Gunderson began to untie the lashes on the mainsail.

"Get on those ropes and hoist up the mainsail," he ordered.

The two policemen moved to the mast and did as instructed. Gunderson loosened the last lash. Then he stepped back. The sail started to rise, unfolding as it went up.

The first policeman grunted. "Something's holding . . ."

He stopped short. Out of the folds of the sail had flopped the lifeless arm of a man.

For a moment the three of them stood without moving. Then, apparently of its own accord, like a slow-motion film, the rest of the body appeared, gradually rolling clear of the sail and, gaining momentum, falling with a thud onto the deck.

His face expressionless, Gunderson looked down at the corpse.

The second policeman, who could not have been long out of his teens, had gone pale. "Is that . . . ?"

The chief nodded. "Sure is. Captain Caleb McCallum has sold his last bowl of clam chowder."

McCallum's body was dressed in just an open-neck shirt and white linen trousers. The shirtfront was perforated with five or six small, blood-encrusted bullet holes.

"Looks like someone really hated him," said the older policeman.

"Lot of people did, son."

Gunderson continued to stare down at the body, rubbing his chin. Almost under his breath he muttered, "So Baxendale's murder *was* a mistake after all."

"What's that, Chief?"

"Oh, nothing. Okay, boys, let's get moving. You know the routine."

"So," Preston said, "it's goodbye for the present."

"I'm afraid so," said Jessica.

They had just returned to Jessica's hotel room.

"Sorry I can't come to see you off tomorrow," he said. "Kitt will be there, of course, but there's no way I can skip an appointment with one of Hollywood's most important producers."

"Of course not. I wouldn't let you, anyway."

"Sorry, too, if I was a bit subdued over dinner, Jess. But as you know, Caleb was an old friend. I knew him when he was a very different man from what he'd become."

"I quite understand. And it was a very pleasant and peaceful evening, all the same."

He gave a wry grin. "Do you realize that after the first minute we didn't discuss the murder at all?"

"No, and we're not going to now. After all, what is there to say? Besides, I'm absolutely *sick* of talking about crime. In fact, in reaction, my next book is likely to be a very mushy love story without the teeniest bit of violence."

"I promise to publish it sight unseen. I'm sure J. B. Fletcher could write a beautiful love story."

"Why, thank you, Preston."

He took her hand. "Jess, despite the insanity that's surrounded our brief acquaintance, these days have been very special to me. You know, for the past several years I've acquired every luxury a man could ask for, but I've been operating on automatic pilot. Automatic banking, automatic security systems, automatic lights—I'm a pampered rich man who does nothing for himself, and I'm miserable. Or at least I have been."

She drew away. "Preston, wait. I do like you a great deal . . ."

"I know. And that's all there is to it, right?"

"So far, yes. As you say, our acquaintanceship has been absurdly brief—and all the circumstances have been so abnormal. Everything's moved much too fast for a widow lady from Maine.''

"I can respect that.''

"Can you?''

"Absolutely. Look, Jess, you and I are going to be joined professionally for a long time. And if something else is destined to come out of this relationship, then so be it. If not, then at least I'll have made a very good friend.''

He kissed her. And at that moment there came a tap on the door.

Preston gave a groan. Jessica called, "Come in.''

The door opened and Roy Gunderson stood in the threshold.

"Sorry to call so late, ma'am,'' he said.

"Not at all, Mr. Gunderson. Won't you come in?''

"Thanks.''

He closed the door behind him, giving a nod to Preston.

"To what do I owe this pleasure, Chief?'' she asked.

"Well, first off, I came to say goodbye. New York City homicide has taken over the McCallum case, so I'm heading back home. Only want to tell you it's been a real pleasure meeting you. Any time you want to horn in on one of my cases, you're welcome.''

"Thank you, Mr. Gunderson; from a professional I take that as a real compliment. And any time you get to Maine, you let me cook you up some lobster stew.''

"I'll do that, Mrs. Fletcher. Thanks.''

"Any developments in the McCallum case, Chief?'' Preston asked.

"Not since the arrest, Mr. Giles.''

They stared blankly at him.

"Arrest?'' Jessica said.

"Who's been arrested?'' Preston asked.

173

It was Gunderson's turn to stare. "I thought you'd heard. It was on all the evening news."

"We haven't seen or heard any news," Preston said. "Tell us who's been arrested?"

"Louise McCallum."

"Louise? Now I wonder . . ." Jessica said slowly.

"You had your doubts about her on Sunday morning, if I remember correctly, ma'am," Gunderson said. "Well, you were right then. We had the wrong victim. But there's no doubt about it this time: Caleb McCallum is positively dead. And there's a very strong case against his wife. Late last night, around midnight, they had a flaming row. It woke the servants, some of whom heard Louise . . . er, Mrs. McCallum . . . threaten to kill Captain McCallum."

Preston interrupted this recital of events. "Mrs. Fletcher doesn't want to get involved, Chief," he said firmly. "She doesn't even want to talk about the case."

Gunderson rubbed his face with a big, beefy hand. "That's a shame."

"Why?" Jessica asked. "You say you have a strong case against Louise. Why should you want me involved?"

"It's not me, ma'am. It's Mrs. McCallum. She wants you to go and see her. She's sure you can clear her. That's the second reason I'm here. To pass on her message: please will you help her?"

"Oh dear." Jessica wearily rubbed her eyes with forefinger and thumb. "What on earth can *I* do?"

Gunderson shrugged. "Frankly, Mrs. Fletcher, I don't know. But as I wanted to tell you so long anyway, I volunteered to give you the message. You see, I felt kinda sorry for her."

"She wants me to go and see her tonight?"

"No, tomorrow will be fine."

Jessica looked at Preston. "I can't refuse, can I?"

"You could, my dear," he said gently. "Many people would."

Jessica gave a sigh. "Very well, Mr. Gunderson, I'll do what I can."

He beamed. "That's swell."

She eyed him shrewdly. "Just why is it swell, Chief?"

He looked a bit embarrassed. "Well, it's—it's just that deep down she seems a real nice lady."

"Why, Mr. Gunderson." Jessica was suddenly mock-coy. "I do believe that beneath that rough exterior beats a heart of gold. And a chivalrous one, to boot."

From his expression, she almost expected him to start scuffing up the rug with his toe, go red, and say, "Aw, shucks."

In fact, all he did was clear his throat. "Don't know about that, ma'am?"

"But you're far from convinced of her guilt, aren't you? Well, I don't think I can actually *do* much. What I will do is listen to the evidence, talk to Louise—and think. If I see any weaknesses in the case against her, any points in her favor, then I'll get in touch with her lawyer. And, of course, I'll tell you as well."

"Reckon I can't ask more than that, Mrs. Fletcher. So you'll be going to see Louise tomorrow?"

"That's a promise. Shall I give her your love?"

Gunderson hesitated. "Better make it my best wishes."

"As you like. And now, Chief, you'd better tell me everything you can about the case. When I see her I must be fully briefed."

Chapter Fifteen

"JESSICA, I swear to you I'm innocent. I did not shoot Caleb. I give you my word."

Louise McCallum spoke with a desperate, pleading urgency.

"My dear Louise," Jessica said quietly, "it's not me you have to convince, you know."

"But I want you to believe me. You do, don't you?"

Jessica didn't answer immediately. But she knew this was a time for complete honesty. "I don't know."

Louise gazed at her in blank dismay. Then, with a gesture of despair, she got to her feet. She went over to the barred window and stared sightlessly out.

Jessica rose. She crossed the bare room, with its drab gray walls and door, its single unshaded light, its plain wooden table and four hard chairs, and joined the other woman.

"My dear," she said, "I'm not saying I *dis*believe you."

"That's all? And I thought we were friends."

"No, we're not."

Louise looked at her coldly. "My mistake, Mrs. Fletcher."

"Now, don't misunderstand me. I only mean that we hardly know each other. We certainly got on well last weekend. We could have become friends. We may yet. But so far, I don't know you nearly well enough to say whether you were capable of shooting your husband. Or to know when you're lying to me. If it's any consolation, my instinct is to believe you."

Louise looked at her for a moment, then managed a sort of smile. "Sorry. My nerves are all on edge."

"Of course they are."

She took Louise by the arm. "Now, come and sit down again and tell me everything."

They went back to the table and seated themselves on opposite sides of it. Jessica felt rather like a lawyer interviewing a client. "Oh, incidentally," she said, "Roy Gunderson sends you his best wishes."

Louise raised her eyebrows. "I wonder why."

"He likes you. He thinks you're a real lady. It's clear he doesn't believe you're guilty."

It was a slight exaggeration of what Gunderson had actually said, but Jessica felt, under the circumstances, it was justified.

Louise looked amazed. "You're joking!"

"Not at all. You have one friend, you see."

"I can sure use all I can get."

"Tell me about your fight with Caleb."

Louise shrugged. "What is there to tell? It was the usual sort of thing. We shouted a lot. It ended with him storming out of the house, yelling that if anybody wanted him he'd be on the yacht."

"The usual sort of thing you say? Yet you threatened to kill him. Was that usual? You've threatened to kill him before?"

"Frequently. But, just between ourselves, I never did. Not once."

"So, it was merely an expression—didn't mean anything?"

"Exactly."

"Could you find witnesses who'd heard you threatening him like that in the past?"

"Well, we didn't usually go at it hammer and tongs in public. But there might be one or two who'd remember. Probably the servants would admit that last night wasn't the first time they'd heard me say it. I don't suppose the police bothered to ask them."

"Well, I should get your attorney to ask them. And anybody else you can think of. The longer ago the better. It's one good point in your favor."

"You talk as if there weren't any others. What about the fact that I actually stood to lose by Caleb's death? Do you know about that?"

"Your prenuptial agreement? Yes. Though I'm afraid it won't carry much weight. The prosecution's case will be that this was a *crime passionnel*—that you weren't thinking rationally."

"That's nonsense!"

"Yet you did chase after him—immediately on top of the fight?"

"Yes. I followed him—maybe ten minutes later—in my own car."

"Why?"

"I wanted to catch him with his floozie. I'd never actually found him with one of them . . . well, let's put it delicately . . . in his arms. I thought this was a good opportunity."

"And you didn't take a gun?"

"No, just a camera. I thought I might get a picture of them."

"You took a camera with you?"

"Yes."

"Where is it now?"

"In the glove compartment of my car, I guess. I don't honestly know. All I remember is having drunk so much I could barely drive. After just a few miles, I pulled off the road to sleep it off." She smiled ironically. "I seem to make a habit of that. Anyway, I never reached the yacht."

"But I should certainly see your attorney has an independent witness check that it's in the glove compartment. It could be another little point in your favor, suggesting the real reason you followed Caleb. And enough little points, all put together . . ."

"Make one big one?"

"Something like that. Tell me, though, what made you think your husband would have a girl with him that night?"

"It was obvious."

"Why?"

"Because earlier he'd told me he was going out to play some poker with the boys. That was absurd. He plays poker Thursday nights—played, I should say—with the same guys every week, and never on the yacht. And they never start as late as that. So of course I knew he had a date. He probably didn't even expect me to believe him."

"Let me get this straight," Jessica said slowly. "He'd already said he was going out *before* you had the fight?"

"That's right."

"Interesting."

Louise looked excited. "It is? Why?"

"Because the impression that's around is that Caleb suddenly decided to go out *as a result* of his fight with you. In other words, no one but you knew he'd be on board the yacht. Now you tell me he had a date there. So at least one other person did know."

"The girl," Louise breathed. "You think *she* could have killed him?"

"Well, it's certainly possible."

"Of course. I should have thought of it before. But my mind's been in such a state . . ."

"Do you know her name?"

Louise shook her head.

"Is it the one who was at the party—Little Red Riding Hood?"

"It could have been, Jessica. I honestly don't know. He changed them like he changed his socks."

"Well, no doubt she can be traced." Jessica looked thoughtful. "The only thing is, it's difficult to see what motive she could have had. Whether she was just a gold digger, or genuinely in love with him, it was obviously in her interest to keep him alive. However, even if she is innocent, she might well have told somebody else about her date. Girls of that type are quite likely to boast about having a millionaire for a sugar daddy—especially to their girl friends."

Jessica stood up. "Louise, I've learned all I need to from you. You've given me a lot to think about. And I feel much surer of your innocence now than when I came in."

Louise gave a smile such as Jessica had not seen from her before. "That's wonderful, Jessica. Thank you."

"I'll report our whole conversation to Roy Gunderson. Now I'm going home. But I promise I'll give this matter a lot of thought. The whole trouble with this case is that it's all been so rushed. There's been no time for reflection. It's had a New York tempo. Well, I'm going to play it over in a Cabot Cove tempo. It might come out much clearer."

Jessica walked along the station platform, in the shadow of the great train. She was possessed by a strange sense of what might be called double *déjà vu*. Twice before she had tried to leave New York City, and twice she had been stopped on the platform.

Surely it couldn't happen again. Well, one thing was sure: Kitt was not going to come running up with disastrous news of Grady this time. For both Kitt and Grady were with her—Grady laden with her suitcase.

At last they reached her sleeper car and Grady deposited the case on the platform.

Kitt took a notebook from her purse and consulted it.

"Just a few last points, Aunt Jess. First, there's been talk of a movie deal. But I'd better warn you not to get your hopes up. These things usually fall through."

"I certainly hope so," Jessica said. "After New York, I know I'm not ready for Hollywood."

"Second, the tape with Barbara Walters will probably be on the air next Friday."

"Thank you, dear. I shall make a point of not being near a TV set. I was terrible."

"I was there. You were fine. Third, the *New York Times* book reporter assigned to cover you—Chris Landon—will be calling by phone for the interview."

"Very well. Now, is that it?"

"That's it."

"I'm free?"

Kitt laughed. "You're free."

"Thank heavens. At last."

"Sorry to have been such a pest."

"You, Kitt, have been a dear."

Jessica embraced her. "I'd never have gotten through it all without you. Now, see that this nephew of mine keeps out of trouble."

"I'll do my best. If he can just curb this unfortunate tendency to get himself arrested."

Jessica turned to Grady and gave him a hug. "And you look after her."

"I will. If she can just curb this unfortunate tendency to find bodies in pools. Sure you have to go, Aunt Jess?"

"Positive."

"And I was certain you'd solve the mystery."

"Well, I couldn't and I didn't and that's that. But I have promised to keep on reflecting."

"Ah," Grady sighed, "like Monsieur Poirot, you sit back and employ ze leetle gray cells."

"I don't know about sitting back. I usually think best when I'm doing something physical but routine, like washing up."

At that moment the conductor swung down from the train. He gave a yell: "All aboard!"

Jessica turned to him. "Why, hullo, Daniel. You again."

"Hi, Mrs. Fletcher. Nice to see you. Leaving at last?"

"Definitely."

Jessica's case was lifted on the train, and she followed it. Kitt handed her a thick wad of newspapers and magazines, Daniel slammed the door, and Grady and Kitt waved and called goodbye.

As the train started to move, Jessica leaned out of the window. "And one other thing, young man," she called. "No surprise telegrams mentioning the word *elopement*. I expect the deed to be done in my parlor."

The train gathered speed. Jessica continued waving until Grady and Kitt were a couple of specks in the distance, then withdrew her head.

Daniel escorted her to her seat and placed her bag on the

rack. "Well, ma'am," he said, "I guess you must have had a fine visit staying all that extra time."

"I could hardly drag myself away. Tell me, Daniel, did your boy hear from the university?"

He beamed. "Yes, ma'am. He starts next September."

"You and your wife must be so proud."

"That we are, ma'am. Well, if there's anything you need, just let me know."

"Thank you. But I don't think I shall. I shall be quite happy to sit here and relax."

He went away. Jessica stared out of the window. She was *not* going to think about the case until she reached home. She just had to have a rest from it.

Distraction. She needed a distraction. She went through the pile of papers and magazines on the seat beside her and selected the *New York Times*.

For ten or fifteen minutes she tried to concentrate on the big national and international news stories—the economy, elections, the Middle East. But her mind kept wandering.

Perhaps something a little less serious . . . Jessica turned to the book section. Now, what was new?

Her eye caught the name Chris Landon. Ah, that was the man who was to interview her. How did he write? she wondered. The column was headed "Book Beat." Jessica soon discovered that he had a nice, informal style. He liked the personal touch —brought in references to the tastes and comments of his family, his friends, his . . .

Jessica stopped short. She blinked. How very odd. It couldn't be!

But yes. There was no mistake.

Slowly Jessica lowered the paper. Thoughts whirled crazily through her mind. All sorts of odd phrases, things seen and not seen, half-absorbed facts . . .

Fancy dress . . . favorite characters . . . Sherlock Holmes . . . Ebenezer Scrooge . . . Edmond Dantes . . . Little Red Riding Hood . . . automatic appliances . . . sonic booms . . . newspapers . . . Chris Landon . . . J. B. Fletcher . . . Justice . . .

Like a kaleidoscope, the pieces came together in Jessica's brain. For the first time they made a pattern, a pattern in which all the elements blended.

If only she could be wrong. But she wasn't. It had to be so . . .

Poor Grady . . .

Chapter Sixteen

FOR a full ten minutes Jessica sat motionless in her seat. She so much wanted to go home. She was tired in body and in mind. It would be so easy just to continue with her journey and forget all about the murders of Dexter Baxendale and Caleb McCallum. Louise would never be convicted. Nor, she was sure, would anyone else. The police investigations would drag on for a few more weeks and then the case would join the great list of unsolved mysteries.

And would that matter? Murders went unsolved all the time—murders worse than these. Both these victims had probably gotten what was coming to them. A lot of people would be better off for their absence from the world. All that she, Jessica Fletcher, had to do was just remain sitting here. It would be so simple. And such a relief.

After all, bringing killers to justice was not her responsibility. It was the job of the police. Nobody could ever blame her or claim she could have done more.

But it was no good. In her heart she knew that to do nothing was impossible. Because Baxendale and McCallum had been human beings. No one had the right to take their lives from them. Besides, a murderer was always dangerous. And one who'd killed twice was especially so. Such a person, if threatened, would probably kill a third time. Perhaps a fourth. Then where might it end?

Therefore, no matter how much she wanted to let this killer go free, she couldn't do it. For however much she tried to rationalize such lack of action, her own conscience would never cease to tell her she was wrong.

Nevertheless, it was with a heavy heart that Jessica got to her feet and went in search of Daniel, to find out which was the train's first stop, and when, from there, she'd be able to get a train back to New York.

On arrival in New York Jessica first phoned Coventry House. There were questions about the night of the party, and about the house, that Preston could answer best. Unfortunately, the office had closed, and the automatic answering machine gave no indication as to where he might be. Nor did the one at his rooms in town. She decided to call the New Holvang house, but found the number was unlisted. To her chagrin, she suddenly realized that in spite of having stayed at the house, she didn't know its number. Kitt would no doubt have it, but Grady, she knew, was meeting Kitt straight from work and they were going out for a long evening.

Jessica could think of nobody else she could ask. Roy Gunderson would probably obtain it for her, but she did not want him to know, at this stage, that she was back in town and on the case.

There seemed no alternative but to go to New Holvang herself. There was one important thing she might be able to discover even without Preston's presence.

First, however, she had time to do a bit of writing.

It was about ten minutes to eight when Jessica's cab

pulled to a halt outside the front door of the Giles mansion. She got out and gazed up at the building. It was in total darkness.

The driver stared out of his window. "Hey, lady, you sure you got the right night?"

"No, not at all sure. Look, I don't think there's much point in ringing the front door bell. I'll go and see if I can find any sign of life in back of the house. Will you please wait?"

"Sure, but remember the meter's running."

"Of course."

She looked around hesitantly, then started toward the side of the house.

Around the corner, without even the glow of the cab's lights, it was completely dark. Jessica groped inside her purse, took out a small flashlight, and switched it on.

By its light she made her way somewhat gingerly to the pool. At the edge of it she stopped for a few seconds, shining her flashlight around and getting her bearings. Then she walked slowly around to the spot at which on Sunday morning she had seen Dexter Baxendale's bloodstains. She bent down. They were fainter but still visible. She straightened and shone her flashlight upward at the ring of unlit lights that surrounded the pool area. She stood quite still for a few minutes. Then she continued on along the side of the pool to the far end. Here was situated an equipment shed, which housed the pool's filtration and heating systems. Jessica went up to the door. It was padlocked.

At that moment out of the darkness she heard a voice.

"Who's there?"

She spun around—and was blinded by the brilliant beam of a powerful flashlight.

"Good grief! Jessica!"

She raised her hand to shield her eyes. "Preston?"

"Yes. My dear, what on earth are you doing here?"

She continued to hold her hand up. "Preston, do you mind?"

"Oh, sorry."

The flashlight was lowered as he came toward her. "Jess, you're supposed to be on your way to Maine."

"I know. I changed my mind."

"But that's wonderful!"

He came right up to her. "I can't say how pleased I am! You can tell me why inside. Come on." He took her arm.

"In a moment. How did you know I was here?"

"I was in my study. The taxi set off a silent alarm as it came up the driveway. I went out to see who it was and spoke to the cabbie. He told me he'd just dropped a lady, who'd disappeared around the side. I couldn't for the life of me think who it might be. Jess, I assume, knowing you, that you have a good reason for prowling around my pool at night. A sort of reconstruction perhaps?"

"Something like that."

He chuckled. "So J. B. Fletcher's still on the case. I might have guessed. Finished now?"

"Not quite. Come with me, Preston."

She led him along the side of the pool and again located the bloodstains with her flashlight. "This is where Baxendale was standing when he was shot, right?"

"Yes, so it seems."

"Stand just here yourself, will you, Preston? Right."

She started to walk away, counting as she did so. She stopped. "And, according to Chief Gunderson, the experts think the shot was fired from about *here*. Correct?"

"Near enough."

"I'm going to switch off my flashlight. Switch yours off too, Preston."

He did so, and heard her voice: "I don't know about you, Preston, but I can't see you at all."

"No, I can't see you either. But what are you driving at?"

"The police believe—and I thought it possible once—that the killer saw an outline of somebody wearing a cape and deerstalker and assumed it was Captain Caleb. But nobody could possibly have seen even *that* much in this sort of light. It would have been just a question of firing blindly into the darkness."

She switched her flashlight on again and walked back to him.

"Well, it obviously wasn't as dark that night," he said. "The moon's waning, remember, and it's overcast now."

"Yes," she said thoughtfully. "But I can't think it would make that much difference."

"Look, let's not stand around here any longer. Come indoors."

"Very well."

He took her arm again and they turned away.

And just then, without any warning, the whole area was suddenly engulfed in brilliant light.

They blinked around, for a moment disoriented. Then Jessica spoke triumphantly: "I thought it might be that! Automatic timing. Am I right?"

Preston was looking dazed. "Yes. Good Lord!"

"What time do they cut off?"

"Er, midnight, I believe. Yes, that's right."

"And the murder took place at eleven-fifteen. So when Baxendale was shot it was as bright as day here."

"That certainly explains a lot."

"Did you let the police know about the lights?"

"No. To tell you the truth, Jess, I'd completely forgotten about that automatic timer. What put you onto it?"

"Something you yourself said about automatic appliances. *I* don't have a pool, of course, but I know some people who do who have just the same arrangement. I tried to call you at the office and ask you about it, but you'd left. I didn't know your number here, or anyone to ask, so I just had to come down and check it out. When I saw the house in darkness, I assumed you weren't here either and decided to have a look myself anyway."

"I'm very glad you did. All the same, I've had enough of this pool now. Let's go inside."

"Aren't you going to turn the lights out now?"

He laughed. "The master switch is in the shed and I don't have a key on me. After all these months, another four hours isn't going to make much difference to my electric bill."

He led her to a side door of the house. "Oh, my taxi!" she exclaimed. "I'd better warn the driver I'm going to be some time."

"I'll pay him off and send him away."

"Oh, Preston, no . . ."

"Why not? When you leave, I can run you to the station. Now, come to my study. That's the coziest place at the moment."

He led her to the pleasant, book-lined room where he had talked to Gunderson on the morning of the murder, and told her to sit down in a big leather arm chair. "Back in a moment."

Jessica sat down, but she didn't relax. She was tense and full of apprehension. What she had to tell him about her deductions was, she knew, going to be an appalling shock; and she just didn't know how he would react.

He came back after about two minutes. "He's gone."

"It's very dark and quiet here, Preston. Where are the servants?"

"I gave them all a few days off. I didn't expect to be here myself. But I decided I had to get away from town for a bit. I can manage quite well on my own." He sat down opposite her. "Now, I'm aching to know what this is all about. I can't believe that it was only a sudden thought about my pool lighting that got you off the train and all the way back to New York."

"No, it wasn't." She took a deep breath. "Preston, I know the identity of the murderer."

His eyes widened. "You mean that? Literally? You really *know?*"

"Yes."

"You have proof?"

"Nothing tangible—but logical proof, yes."

"You'd better tell me who it is," he said quietly.

"I hate to say it, Preston. It's going to be an even bigger shock to you than it was to me. But I'm afraid it's Kitt."

For a second or two Preston sat staring at her without speaking. "You can't be serious."

"I'm sorry. But . . . ." She trailed off.

He stood up suddenly and took several aimless steps about the room. "I . . . I just don't believe it."

"I didn't expect you to—at first. But it all fits in. Just listen."

With obvious reluctance, he sat down again.

Jessica began her recital of events. "Ashley Vickers said that for several months her relationship with the Captain had

191

been on a strictly business basis. I believe that. Now, he only met his latest girl friend, Tracy Ellison, the night of the party. He must have, because he told Chief Gunderson he didn't even know her second name. But he hasn't been without a girl during that intervening period. Ask Louise. She says he changed his girls like he changed his socks.''

Preston broke in, his voice incredulous: ''You're saying *Kitt* was that girl?''

Jessica bowed her head. ''Until Little Red Riding Hood—Tracy—pushed her out. Kitt saw it happening the night of the party. She's a proud girl. She wouldn't stand for it. I believe she confronted McCallum that night and he told her they were through. She went out to the pool area, probably just to be alone, and—as she believed—saw him there. The gun had been left lying around; she picked it up and shot him. Though, actually, of course, she shot Baxendale. My, but she did a good acting job the next morning, feigning such shock at finding the body. Or perhaps it wasn't all acting. Perhaps something about the corpse made her realize that it wasn't McCallum—that she'd shot the wrong man. If so, her shock was no doubt genuine.''

Jessica paused and moistened her lips before continuing.

''I think McCallum guessed the truth. But he had no proof, and probably wouldn't have given her away to the police anyway. However, he either told her of his belief, or somehow she realized he knew. He then presented a tremendous threat to her. She couldn't relax, knowing that at any time he could give her away. She had to kill him.

''I know from Louise that Caleb had a date on the yacht the night of his death. I believe Kitt called him, pretending to be Tracy, and arranged to meet him there. She got there ahead of him and lay in wait. Then, when he arrived . . ." Jessica stopped.

Preston lowered his head and held it between his hands. She watched him silently. At last he looked up. It was plainly an effort, but he spoke calmly and quietly. "You say you have logical proof of all this. What, exactly?"

"It consists of things Kitt said, things she knew which she couldn't have known unless she were guilty; how they tie up with things Louise said, Grady said. It's all very complicated. Difficult to explain clearly in words."

She reached into her purse and took out an unsealed envelope. "I've written it all out, in the form of a long letter to Chief Gunderson. As soon as I leave here I'm going to mail it."

Preston looked at the envelope, then lifted his eyes to hers. He said heavily: "Jess, don't send that letter."

"I must, Preston. Do you think I'm not tempted— desperately—to let things be? But I can't let the girl get away with two murders. I can't let her marry Grady. Double murderers don't stop at two. I *must* send it."

"I wouldn't try to stop you if I thought she was guilty. But she isn't."

"You can't know that."

"I do know it."

"Your belief in her character isn't knowledge, Preston."

"It's not that. I know it because . . ."

He stopped. He'd gone very pale. "I know it, Jessica, because . . . *I* murdered Baxendale and McCallum."

The only sound was the tick of an antique silver clock on the mantelpiece. There was no movement. For what seemed a long time they sat as though figures in a tableau.

Then Jessica let her breath out very slowly. "I see," she said softly.

"You don't seem surprised."

"I'm not."

He stared at her in amazement. "You're telling me you *knew?*"

"Yes."

"But . . . but"—he was stammering—"all that about Kitt . . ."

"A lot of fiddle-faddle. I didn't believe a word of it."

"But that letter . . ."

"Read it." She held the envelope out to him.

He took it with a hand that shook only slightly and removed several sheets of paper covered with small, neat handwriting. He unfolded them.

Dear Chief Gunderson, he read. *It is with deep regret I have to inform you that without question the murderer of Dexter Baxendale and Caleb McCallum is Preston Giles. My grounds for this statement are as follows . . .*

Preston read no more. He looked at Jessica, his face a study of bafflement. "But why?" he said blankly.

"Why did I accuse Kitt? Because I couldn't bear to accuse *you* to your face, Preston. Perhaps because I'm a coward. I wanted to give you a chance to confess."

He got to his feet again. He went slowly to the window, pulled open the drapes, and stared out into the darkness. With his back to her he said lifelessly: "How did you know?"

"You made one mistake—and only one. It was that phone call on the night of the party."

"Phone call?"

"When Ashley and I came into the kitchen to get some

things to clean her dress, you were on the phone. You mentioned my name. After you hung up, you told me the caller had been a *New York Times* reporter called Chris Landon. You said he wanted to interview me, but that you'd agreed to see him. I thought nothing of it. But today on the train I was reading Chris Landon's column. And halfway through it Chris Landon refers to . . . her *husband*. Yes, Chris Landon is a woman. And you didn't know that. At first I just couldn't understand it. Then I remembered how one paper had referred to me as *Mr.* J. B. Fletcher. Because it's nearly always *men* who designate themselves only by their initials, the paper had assumed *I* was a man.

"My guess is that Chris Landon had in fact called earlier, but you hadn't spoken to her, only been given a written message. You just assumed Chris Landon was a man. When I overheard you mention my name on the phone and you were forced to say whom you'd been speaking to, you said the first name that came into your head. But I realized on the train that you must have been lying—you'd obviously never spoken to Chris Landon at all. I couldn't think *why* you'd have lied.

"I'd been idly puzzling for a long time over something else—something Baxendale said to you about your being dressed as the Count of Monte Cristo. He said it after very obviously catching sight of that figure of Blind Justice in your bedroom. It seemed quite irrelevant, yet oddly meaningful. It was as if something had suddenly clicked into place with him.

"And then, while on the train, I linked the two facts— Baxendale's words and your lie. I realized his words had been a sort of secret message to you, though I don't think you grasped the fact at the time. It had been he on the phone.

He asked you, didn't he, to meet him outside that night? You went.''

She paused. Preston didn't react. "Go on," he said without turning around.

"It was the first time I'd suspected you and I was horrified. But I had to follow it up. Could you have shot Baxendale deliberately in that sort of light? And then I thought of my friends' automatic pool lights. Surely any such automatic gadget that was available, *you* would have. And when those lights came on, any lingering doubts I might have had vanished. For frankly, Preston, I don't for one moment believe you forgot about that automatic timing. You're just not the sort of person to forget a thing like that. You knew it had been bright as day by the pool when Baxendale was killed. He was shot from the front, from close range. That was the big flaw in my argument which you didn't spot, when I was accusing Kitt just now: the fact that nobody for one second could have mistaken Baxendale's face for McCallum's. Baxendale was the target all along. Yet you let the police—and me—assume the light was poor by the pool, and that perhaps Baxendale had been shot in error. You even went so far as to dress the body in the Holmes costume, which you knew the Captain had discarded, in order to foster the belief that Caleb was the intended victim. You feared if the police investigated Baxendale's affairs too closely they would eventually trace some connection with you. Tell me, Preston, am I right?''

He turned around, came back to his chair, and sat down. "Many years ago," he began, "I was betrayed by three partners in a business venture. An apartment house we'd built collapsed. Several people were killed. Although I had nothing to do with the construction end, I was made the scapegoat. They got off free and I was sentenced to fifteen years in prison. After two years I managed to escape. Don't ask the details—but the police assumed I'd died in the attempt.''

"Like the Count of Monte Cristo," Jessica said.

"As you well know, my favorite fictional character. Well, not everyone was convinced I was dead. A hotshot detective, third grade, had a hunch I was still alive. He was even more positive when, over the next couple of years—like the Count of Monte Cristo—I financially destroyed my three ex-partners from a safe distance. He looked for a while longer, but eventually gave up. Saturday was the first time I'd seen him in twenty-two years. He'd changed his name, as I had, and I didn't recognize him, though he did, as I soon discovered, recognize me. He must have thought his ship had come home with a vengeance: two possible sources of big money hit on within a few minutes—Caleb's real estate report and dirt on me. Naturally, he wasn't going to risk losing the report—which I'm sure he had no intention of returning to Caleb, incidentally—so he took that back to his car and locked it in. Then, deciding to strike while the iron was hot, he went to a pay phone and called me. That was the first time I realized who he was. He insisted I meet him by the pool at eleven o'clock. Blackmail was his game. He said he had a thick dossier on me in his office. Baxendale threatened to tell everybody who I was if I didn't meet him. He was especially insistent he would tell *you,* as though he'd somehow sensed during that few minutes he was with us in my room how I felt for you. That was how I happened to mention your name—just as you came into the room.

"I couldn't let him do it to me, Jess. I went to the rendezvous. But I took the skeet gun with me. The rest you know.''

"You took a tremendous risk," she said.

"Not so great as the risk of losing everything. And there was always the chance the sound of the gun would be taken for a sonic boom. It was just bad luck there were no flights that night. So those neighbors of mine were able to pinpoint the exact time it happened. If they hadn't, *nobody* would have had an alibi and there'd have been many more suspects for the police to check out.

"Not that it's really mattered, as things have turned out."

He sounded very, very tired.

He looked at her steadily. "He was a slimy blackmailer, Jess. He threatened to destroy my life. Morally, it was a case of self-defense."

"Even if I could bring myself to believe that, Preston, there's no way you can justify the murder of Caleb McCallum."

"Caleb wasn't much of a human being either. In killing him I did a good turn to Louise, and to the next young woman he would have taken up and then dumped."

"But he didn't deserve *killing,*" she said fiercely "And you didn't do it for Louise, or anybody else. You did it to divert suspicion from yourself, by switching the investigation away from Baxendale—proving his death was just a mistake."

"Oh, that was part of it, but not all, by any means. You see, Caleb had known for years I had some sort of guilty secret. We were great buddies at one time, and once or twice I probably spoke a bit too freely. For a long time it didn't matter, for whatever his faults he was a loyal friend. But then, after Baxendale's death, he became suspicious of me."

"He did?"

"Yes. Remember, he knew Baxendale, and probably guessed he wouldn't be above a little blackmail. He also knew Baxendale had seen me, had left the house and gone to his car, and then come back. He realized that once Baxendale had gotten away from the house with that real estate report, it would take something special to make him return. Finally, Caleb was aware *I* knew he'd taken off the Holmes costume and put it in the closet. Knowing that I was vulnerable to blackmail, it didn't take him long to start suspecting me. After you saw him on his yacht that day, he called me and asked me to come to his office late that afternoon."

"And you went. You mentioned it."

"Most of the staff had left by the time I got there. Caleb was very odd. Didn't in so many words accuse me of the murder, but made it pretty clear he wasn't in much doubt. He didn't actually say he was going to the police, but I couldn't possibly take the risk of letting him.

"While I was there that girl Tracy phoned. Quite openly he made a date to see her on the yacht that night. Then he let me go—still giving no clue what he meant to do. That evening I phoned Tracy's apartment, spoke to her roommate, said I was Caleb, and canceled the date. Later after you and I'd had supper with Kitt and Grady, I drove out to Bayside, boarded the *Chowder King*, and waited for him. And—well, you know what happened."

"I know you let Louise be arrested—for your crime."

"Jess, that was a nightmare! How on earth could I have known that that night, of all nights, she and Caleb were going to have a fight, that people would overhear her threaten to kill him, and that she'd drive off after him and disappear for the rest of the night? However, as I knew she was innocent, I couldn't believe she'd be found guilty. I was tremendously relieved when Gunderson doubted her guilt and you agreed to take a hand. All the same, if the worst had happened, I swear to you I wouldn't have let her be convicted.''

''I believe you, Preston. I'm sure, you see, in spite of all this, that in your own way you're a man of honor.''

Suddenly, for the first time, Jessica broke down. She turned her head away. ''Oh, Preston, she said in a distraught voice, ''I'm so angry I don't know whether to scream or cry. All the way to the train station today I kept thinking about you. Twice I nearly turned around and came back. And then, when I saw that newspaper, when I realized . . .''

He stood up, moved across to her chair, and put his hand on her shoulder. ''I'm sorry, Jess. I truly am.''

She straightened, dived into her purse, took out a handkerchief, dabbed vigorously at her eyes, and blew her nose.

''Well, Preston, what are you going to do now?''

''The question is, my dear, what are you going to do? Go to the police, I suppose?''

''I hope I shan't have to.''

''You mean you expect me to give myself up? Well, as no doubt you've already told someone else of your deductions, I have little choice.''

''But I haven't.''

''Then you've left a letter with an attorney or somebody.''

''I haven't done that, either.''

He looked flabbergasted. "You mean . . ."

"I mean that nobody but you and I knows of your guilt, Preston. Only the taxi driver, who I'm sure didn't recognize me, is aware I've been here. I've seen not a soul who knows me since I got off the train this afternoon."

He straightened up and stared down at her. "You do realize what you're saying? That I could kill you here and now; and very probably get away with it—as well as the other two murders."

"Yes."

"And you talk of my taking a risk! A few minutes ago you said double murderers don't stop at two, remember?"

"I remember. And I'm staking my life on my firm belief that you, Preston, will not harm *me.*"

Jessica's heart was beating very fast. She didn't know whether she looked frightened, but she certainly felt it.

He continued to gaze down at her. Every muscle of his body was tense, and she knew beyond doubt that the temptation to kill her was very real. She had never been in greater danger than now.

Then the moment passed. As if by a conscious effort he relaxed, and it was as though a pressure gauge had suddenly been turned down. He went across the room to a small cocktail cabinet, poured himself a glass of whiskey, and downed it in one go.

"Do you want a drink?" he asked.

"No, thank you."

He put down the glass and returned to his chair. "You're right, of course. I could never hurt you, Jess. You can walk out of here unhindered whenever you like."

"And you? Will you go to the police and tell the truth?"

"What will you do if I say no? Go yourself?"

"I don't think I could bring myself actually to go into a police station and inform on you. I shall mail my letter to Chief Gunderson."

He was silent. Then: "You won't need to do that."

"You will give yourself up?"

"I promise I'll let Gunderson have a full confession. And for good measure, I'll see he gets your letter as well. I'm sure it lays out the facts much more succinctly than I shall be able to."

Jessica hesitated for only a moment. Then she bowed her head. "Very well. Your word is good enough for me, Preston."

He stood up, walked to the phone, dialed, and asked for Chief Gunderson. He listened for a moment, then hung up. "He'll be here in ten minutes."

He got to his feet and went over to her. "Another time, Jess, a different place, we might have had something."

She took his hand. "We might indeed."

He drew her to him, took her in his arms, and held her close for a moment. Then he pulled away, put his hands on her shoulders, and looked into her eyes.

"Forgive me, Jess?"

"What is there for *me* to forgive?" She turned aside. Her voice broke. "I . . . I think . . . if you don't mind, I'll walk down the driveway and wait for the Chief there."

"As you wish, my dear."

"Don't see me out."

"Very well."

Without looking at him again, she walked quickly to the door and opened it.

"Goodbye, Preston."

The door closed behind her.

"Goodbye, Jessica," he said softly.

But she didn't hear.

Chapter Seventeen

"AUNT Jess, how did you hatch that story you told Preston Giles about Kitt?"

"The whole thing was just a product of my overfertile imagination."

She took Kitt by the hand. "I'm so sorry, my dear, for maligning your character in that way to Preston. It was just the only way I could think of to make him tell me the truth."

They were in Kitt's apartment. Grady and Jessica had stopped off on their way to the station for Jessica to say a final goodbye.

"Oh, I don't mind in the least," Kitt said airily. "In fact"—she tossed her head at Grady—"I'm quite flattered that anybody would believe all that of me."

Grady shook his head sorrowfully. "Hopeless. Just a natural-born delinquent, this girl."

Kitt turned to Jessica. "And speaking of natural-born delinquents, why did you phone asking me for Tracy Ellison's number earlier?"

"I wanted to clear up all the loose ends. That anonymous phone call to the police about the murder on the yacht. I had my own idea. And I was right. Tracy, suspecting she'd been ditched for another girl, made her way to the yacht club that night to try to find out. She waited on the quay about fifty yards away. Preston must have been there by then, but she saw the Captain arrive and go aboard. A few minutes later she saw and heard . . . well, not enough to know exactly what had happened, or identify the murderer, but enough to know Caleb had been shot. She panicked and ran away. But later she phoned the police. She spoke in a whisper so they wouldn't identify her voice as a woman's.''

"Must have been a terrifying experience for her," Grady said. "Poor kid."

"I shouldn't waste too much sympathy on her," Jessica assured him. "I don't think she's exactly overwhelmed with grief. In fact, she's already collaborating with a ghostwriter for some scandal sheet on an article to be called 'My Love for Cap'n Caleb.' As she said to me, 'A girl's got to take care of herself.' ''

"Things seem to be working out quite well all around," he said. "Ashley's making a deal with the D.A. that will keep her out of jail. Brill will probably get a comparatively short sentence. Louise is out of prison and on the wagon. *And* is so very grateful to Roy Gunderson, who is now a frequent caller at her house. Finally, J. B. Fletcher vindicates her nephew, solves the mystery, gives her book a tremendous boost of publicity—and builds herself an overnight reputation as a crackerjack amateur detective. Highly satisfactory.''

"For everybody but you, my dear," she said sympathetically. "Do you know, almost the first thought that occurred to me when I realized Preston might be guilty was, 'poor Grady.' Just when he'd promised to help find you a job in publishing."

"Oh, don't worry about me, Aunt Jess. There are always openings for guys like me: brilliant, dynamic, charming . . ."

". . . modest, unassuming," Kitt murmured.

He put his arm around her waist. "Besides, we're thinking of pooling our talent and experience and going into partnership."

"Oh, doing what?"

"Producing a book. How does this grab you as an eye-catching title? *History and Practice of Accounting in the Clam Chowder Industry.* Think it'll make the charts?"

"Very possibly," Jessica said. "But I shouldn't bank on selling the movie rights."

She looked at her watch. "Well, if you're taking me to the station, we'd better get moving."

"Do you think it's really worth the bother this time?"

"Grady, this time I *am* going home. And I am not coming back to this city. Not next month, not next year. Never."

"Point taken," he said.

She turned to Kitt. "Goodbye, Kitt, dear. And again, thanks for everything."

"Thank *you*, Aunt Jess."

They embraced and a minute later Jessica and Grady left.

At the station Jessica said: "I seem to have spent half my life on this platform lately."

"Well, let's hope this is the last time. Tell me, Aunt Jess, how do you feel now?"

"Still rather shattered."

"You really like Preston, don't you?"

"Yes, I really like him. Oh, Grady, if I hadn't been such

a terrible busybody, if only I'd let it be . . ." She took a grip on herself. "Anyway, now I've had enough. Enough murders, enough suspects, enough puzzles. I'm not even sure I'm going to write another book."

"Sure you are. And I'll be the first one to read it."

She smiled. "Well, we'll see."

She kissed him and boarded the train. Then she turned and looked out of the window. She was about to say goodbye, when suddenly she heard a voice calling.

"Aunt Jess—wait!"

Flying down the platform toward them was Kitt.

Grady gave an exclamation as the girl came running up to them. "Kitt, what on earth's the matter?"

She was panting for air. "Aunt Jess, the police have just phoned my apartment. They've been trying to find you all morning. They won't say it, but I think they need help."

"Help from *me?*"

She nodded. "The bodies of two dead wrestlers were found this morning at Madison Square Garden—lying side by side in the middle of the ring. One had been stabbed. The other drowned."

"No!" Jessica said. "Absolutely not!"

At that moment the train started to move.

Kitt called breathlessly, "They said they're sure there's a logical explanation, but . . ."

Jessica cut her off. "Grady, *tell* her. Goodbye, children. Be sure to write—and remember, I expect to see you soon."

She gave a wave and withdrew into the train.

She made her way to her seat, sank gratefully down on it,

and closed her eyes. She'd made it! Soon she'd be back in Cabot Cove, and . . .

Jessica's eyes opened. She sat up and stared blankly ahead of her. One had been stabbed. And the other . . .

"Drowned?" she said out loud.